DANCING WITH DETECTIVE DANGER

AEGAR INVESTIGATIONS

LYNN CRANDALL

Praise for award-winning author Lynn Crandall

"Ms. Crandall promises us a dance with danger and this story delivers. The detective is icing for our cake." Amazon for *Dancing with Detective Danger*

"*Dancing with Detective Danger* is a fast-paced read and filled with plot twists. I didn't want to put it down!" Amazon

"It's hard to tell if this is a romantic thriller or a thrilling romance, but readers won't be able to forget the interesting characters, and their heart stopping voyage to an everlasting love delivered by Ms. Crandall with a masterful stroke." InDtale Magazine for *Then There Was You*

"A full throttle, new take on the legends and myths surrounding Atlantis. Touch Me forces readers to hold on for dear life and invites them to enjoy the ride." InDtale for *Touch Me*

"A well written story of suspense, drama, danger, evil, and two people falling in love..." Amazon for *Two Days Until Midnight*

"Lynn Crandall held my interest from start to finish with unexpected surprises and a satisfying story. Her characters are alive and easy to relate to as they struggle with inner stories that affect their lives—real issues people live with daily. An engaging plot made it hard to put the book down.

"There is a broadness in this book's world where emotions and awareness of life beyond the physical are acknowledged. Her characters effectively illustrate the struggles of finding balance in the battle between self-protection and reaching for help while fearing to need it. The issue of being walled off to feel safe from the danger of being open and vulnerable are a familiar human experience. I'd like to follow this cast of characters in new adventures."

Dancing with Detective Danger
by
Lynn Crandall

ACKNOWLEDGMENTS

Thank you to my favorite detectives, technology experts, and therapist for their excellent and willing help in building a story with true to life and flawed by redeemable characters. I also want to thank my family and friends, especially HiDee Ekstrom, for their support and encouragement, and members of my writing group. I also am grateful to Dar Albert of Wicked Smart Designs for her amazing cover work. And a special thank you to my husband for always being there with patience and encouragement.

CHAPTER 1

*E*ven very renowned professional private investigators have a bad day now and then.

At twenty-six-years old, Sterling Aegar knew in her heart that she and her sister qualified as professional PIs and serious career women. Sometimes things simply happen. Not everything can be controlled and unexpected things are bound to occur, she assured herself. Still, she silently surveyed the scene of her latest case and wondered if anything else could go wrong this morning.

The woman's nude body lying submerged in the nearly over-flowing tub looked oddly serene. Her eyes seemed almost peaceful and her hair floated like a blond halo around her head.

"Nice doggie," her sister, Lacey Aegar, cooed, but the large German shepherd staring at her continued to growl nastily.

"Look at those teeth!" Though her heart beat emphatically, Sterling barely moved her lips as she spoke under her breath to her sister, not wanting to draw attention from the snarling dog. "Well, sis, what does the private investigator's manual suggest we do at a time like this? I seem to have left mine back at the office."

"As if such a manual exists." Sterling glanced around the marble-floored bathroom, looking for something, anything, to protect herself

"

and her sister from the angry dog. Her gaze paused at the sunken tub adorned with elegant brass fixtures.

Warning flags had gone off inside Sterling's head from the moment she and her sister walked through the opened front door of the pricey condo. Especially attuned to her gut instinct, Sterling always paid attention to its prompting. Sometimes it took time to play out, and following the thread took patience and persistence. Yet a keen awareness and respect for instinct and intuition was something she knew stood her well in many investigations, so she didn't take the uneasy feeling lightly. The warnings this morning seemed to say, *Beware. Something about this new case is not as it seems.* So finding a dead woman in the course of a standard surveillance and infidelity investigation was not only completely unexpected, it confirmed the instinctive suspicion Sterling felt thrumming in her middle.

"Why do these things happen to us?" Sterling spouted softly, bringing her attention back to the threat of the moment -- the angry Shepherd standing poised beside the tub.

"Because, sister dear, we are cursed." Lacey appeared quite at ease.

Sterling frowned at her. "Quit teasing. This is serious."

"I'm not teasing. The curse is from Mom's side of the family," she said. "Probably some great-great-great grandfather spit on someone's grave and bingo, generations suffer a curse. Although, the case could be argued today that we're lucky. Mr. Teeth could have attacked us at the front door."

"Lacey!" Sterling hissed. "We've got to do something. We can't stand here all day. That dog is no doubt guarding his beloved mistress, and he doesn't seem to have any sense of humor about us barging in."

"Yeah, poor fella. Do you think he understands that she's dead?"

Sterling rolled her eyes. "Why is it people always feel more compassion for animals than for humans? I mean, the woman is dead, Lacey. And excuse me, I'll wait until later to offer the dog my condolences, if you don't mind."

"Hmm, you've got a good point. Let's just back out of the room."

Sterling swallowed hard, held her breath, and glanced at Lacey. "Okay, now...slowly."

Sterling took one step back simultaneously with Lacey, but the dog leaned menacingly toward them, bared his teeth, and growled a warning.

"Isn't that just like a man," Lacey said. "He doesn't want us to get too close, but he doesn't want us to leave, either."

"Will you quit with the quips?"

"Maybe he doesn't like my outfit."

"Yeah, that's it. He's offended by your clothes," Sterling teased. She rolled her eyes again at Lacey, who was dressed stylishly in a denim micro-mini skirt over black leggings and a simple grey tunic. Several delicate, long silver chains layered under a metallic bohemian scarf completed her look.

"There is nothing wrong with my outfit, little sister," Lacey proclaimed.

"Okay, big sister. It wasn't me who made the suggestion."

"I'm perfectly comfortable with my style of dressing. I'm only thirty years old. I can have fun with my clothes. You should lighten up, too." Lacey slanted her head in Sterling's direction, as though suggesting her sister's clothing choice left something to be desired. "Now, let's concentrate on getting out of here. I'll distract Mr. Teeth and you try to get away."

"Are you nuts? Do you know what teeth like that can do to your skin? I'm not leaving you."

"Right. Well…" Lacey glanced around anxiously. "I'm sure there are plenty of toxic sprays or sharp objects in here somewhere, but I don't hardly dare move, even if I would be willing to hurt him in that way.

"Oh, no, we wouldn't want to hurt the vicious dog. Don't you have something in your purse we could distract him with? Something to eat? You're always munching on something."

"What a brilliant idea!" Slowly, Lacey opened her purse and drew out a bag.

"A sandwich?" Sterling knew she shouldn't be surprised, but the sight of two pieces of bread and some meat coming out of her sister's purse seemed a bit odd even for Lacey. "Okay, you can fling it out the door and down the hall away from us. When he goes after it we'll head out the door. On three, throw it and run."

"On four. You know how I hate odd numbers."

Sterling sighed. "You're such a mess! Okay, on four. One, two, three, four!"

Lacey aimed for the hallway and miraculously, the dog immediately ran after the bait, a limp slowing him a little. Sterling exchanged a quick knowing look with Lacey.

Before the dog had a chance to reconsider, Sterling followed her sister through the front door and down the street to where Lacey's compact car sat parked on the side of the road.

Safely inside the vehicle, Lacey turned to Sterling. "That was fun," she said, a wry smile lifting her lips. "Are you okay?"

"Sure. Are you?"

"As soon as my heart rate slows I'll let you know," Lacey joked.

Sterling's attention landed idly on a robin pecking at blades of new spring grass and she imagined the dog already back beside his owner. Deliberately, she set aside the uneasiness churning in her stomach. She picked up her cell phone from the car seat and punched the numbers for the Laurelwood Police station.

FROM THE STUCCO-COLORED leather couch and leaded glass coffee table smartly arranged in front of the stone fireplace, to the fine art prints hanging on the walls, the living room of the deceased woman spoke of money -- lots of it. With the insistent barking of the confined German shepherd echoing from another room, Sterling stood watching the plain-clothes officers and detectives working the scene, her thoughts drifting in all directions.

This could have been her life -- working a crime scene with fellow police officers. She'd fulfilled her childhood vow to herself to honor her father by following in his footsteps and graduated from the Police Training Institute at the top of her class. With single-minded dedication, she'd picked up the cause: Fighting to keep the city safe from the kind of scum that had killed her father.

Putting in her time as a beat cop on the Laurelwood streets was part of the job, so she'd issued her share of parking tickets and speeding citations. She'd put her all into it right from the start, but always with her sights set on making detective. To some day, as quickly as possible, get knee deep in fighting the bad guys. It was a palpable impatience ramping up her ambition. But it wasn't an ambition solely to make a name for herself or rise through the ranks. Sterling wanted…needed to make a difference in her own way…to ensure innocent people didn't suffer the needless pain that tore at her family after her father's murder. Policing the streets helped calm the inescapable sorrow.

She searched the room for someone who looked in charge and finally landed on one officer. "Excuse me, you've gotten our statement, I'd like to leave."

Pulling up from his scrutiny of an area of the living room, the officer stared for a moment at Sterling, then cleared his throat. "I'm not in charge and we're waiting for the detective who is. He should be arriving soon." The officer turned back to his work, clearly dismissing her.

Back in her corner of the room, Sterling's stomach knotted as her thoughts about her past naturally turned to Ben. Ben Kirby had been a part of all that from the moment they'd met on the job. As an undercover detective on the Drug Task Force, he'd shown her the edge. He didn't merely patrol the city, he prowled it, daring the dealers and runners to make a move. And when they did, he was there to pounce on them without mercy. Ben went after his targets with no thought of a safety net. Get the job done, take down the low-lifes, get them into a cell. Granted, the mid-size, Midwestern town of Laurelwood was not a hotbed of evil, but it did have its share of crime. And Ben didn't give a second thought to laying his life on the line for the sake of justice.

But that was history, she thought with an internal shrug. Sterling drew in a deep breath and checked her wristwatch uneasily as the officers made their way through the evidence collection. Sterling hadn't seen or spoken to Ben in two years, so thoughts of him had no place in her mind, she told herself, letting the hard, familiar ache in her heart bury itself again.

She glanced again at her watch, then over at Lacey who nonchalantly fingered her curly red hair as she stood talking with two of the investigators.

Sterling's agitation was growing, knowing she and her sister had already relayed to the officers the details of finding the dead woman. She felt fidgety, ready to move on, get out of this place. It was prompting thoughts from her past that did no good to rehash.

A detective caught Sterling's eye and walked across the room. "Ms. Aegar, I want to go over this again. You and your sister found the body at eleven a.m., correct?"

Sterling tapped her foot. "Yes, that's correct," she said with forced calm. Patience was not her strong suit, but she didn't care. Pressure inside her was building. The walls were drawing in on her. "Like I said, we're private investigators. We were on an assignment. We rang the doorbell. No one answered." Deliberately, she drew out the words, wondering how many times the simple story needed to be spelled out for this guy.

"So you two just went in anyway."

His tone of voice made her bridle. "I told you, we were on assignment. We rang the doorbell, we knocked, no one answered, and in fact, the door stood slightly ajar. We went in. We looked around. When we walked into the bathroom we found the woman and the dog."

"That's when you saw the body submerged in the bathtub."

"Bingo! I think you're finally getting the picture," Sterling exclaimed. She didn't attempt to hide her impatience.

"You know I could book you on breaking and entering. What kind of an assignment were you working on?"

Sterling squared her shoulders and narrowed her eyes. "You know that's confidential."

"Are you saying you're not willing to cooperate with the police?"

"Is there some point to all of this interrogation?" Sterling hedged, for no other reason than this guy's superior attitude was making her skin crawl. Normally, cooperating with the local law enforcement was SOP, a logical and necessary standard operating procedure. But she was having a bad day and this guy needed to be taken down a notch. "Do you think I'm lying? Maybe you'd like to frisk me to make sure I'm not withholding a murder weapon, or something." She heard footsteps coming up behind her but kept her glare pointed at the officer.

"Don't bluster at the officer, Sterling. He's just doing his job."

The deep voice at her shoulder startled her so intensely her breath froze in her chest, but Sterling squelched her reaction. Deliberately, she turned to face the man. "Hello, Ben. What are you doing here?" She'd forgotten how much taller he stood above her. His dark hair was shorter than two years ago, making his cobalt blue eyes more vivid and his strong jaw more imposing.

"I work investigations now." His smiled reached out effortlessly and grabbed her unwilling heart, but Ben seemed unaware.

"Really? That explains the suit." Sterling turned back to the officer, struggling to keep her voice steady, emotionless, despite the seismic quakes coursing through her body. "Do you have any other questions?"

"Well--"

"We won't be needing you any further right now, Sterling," interrupted Ben, clearly the detective in charge. "But if we need to get in touch with you, where would we find you?"

As if he doesn't know. "Our detective agency's number is in the book." While it was true that Ben hadn't ever actually stepped through her agency's door, if she knew anything at all, she knew he'd kept tabs on her office location if nothing else. That was just the kind of cop he was.

"You and your sister are still in the private investigating business?" Innocence dripped from Ben's richly masculine voice.

"Ben Kirby!" Lacey stepped up and warmly wrapped her arms around him.

"Hi, Lacey."

It was so "Lacey" to walk right up to Ben as though no time had passed and nothing had changed. But Sterling stifled a grin at Ben's obvious discomfort with the display of affection in front of his fellow officers, his arms stiff at his sides. "Ben's working investigations now, Lacey."

"Well, that's good, if it's what you want. It's nice to see you, Ben. It's a wonder we haven't bumped into you before. But, then, Sterling and I don't usually run across dead bodies in the course of our work. Our cases tend to be more like backgrounds and investigating insurance and disability claims and--"

"Ben was just asking about our work," Sterling interrupted. *Leave it to Lacey to lay out all the boring details in the first four seconds.*

"How nice." Lacey shot Sterling a quizzical look.

"And I was just telling him that Aegar Investigating is thriving. So, we better get to the office, Lacey. We have work to do." With one parting look up into Ben's face, Sterling led her sister outside.

"Geez, sis, what was your hurry? Feeling a little uncomfortable? I can see why. Ben looks great. And the electricity between the two of you –- wow! It was unmistakable."

Sterling took in a deep breath and slowly let it out, letting her sister ramble on as the two walked to the car. "Don't start with me, Lacey. You know there's nothing between Ben and me."

"Okay, okay. Don't get all edgy. I just think it's interesting that after all this time we run into him." Lacey smiled a whisper of a smile, suggesting she wasn't giving up at all.

"I don't think it's one bit interesting." Sterling climbed into the passenger seat of Lacey's car and deliberately avoided looking at the condo as her sister started the engine. "What is interesting is the fact that we stumbled into a murder scene. It's the first really exciting case we've come across in a long time."

"Work. That's all you want to talk about." Lacey rolled her eyes. "It's in the hands of the police, now."

"I suppose you're right." Sterling sighed. "It doesn't hurt to wish, does it?"

"I know you miss police work. You can't help but resonate with the thrill of the edge. It's in your blood." Lacey eyed Sterling with sisterly understanding.

"I don't miss police work." Sterling was quick to stomp on the suggestion. "I just wish for a little more action at our agency. A little more of righting wrongs. Sometimes it's not a clear line between the good guys and the bad guys with what we often do. I wish—"

"Listen, if you're going to wish for something, make it for something good and definitely doable, like a white chocolate café mocha, Vente. Mmm…I can taste it now."

Sterling shook her head. "You really know how to dream big."

BEN STOOD behind the richly embroidered slate-colored drapes at the condo's living room window and discreetly watched Sterling walk to the car as he shuffled paperwork through his fingers. Her petite frame, dressed in a slim gray suit, pulled his attention as though he had no control.

That's the way it was with her. He hadn't seen her for two years, but all during that time he'd been unable to will her out of his thoughts for very long. Seeing her up close and feeling her presence stirred up old feelings inside him. During the time they'd been together, the terrible aloneness he'd grown to live with had vanished. It hadn't mattered that before she came along he'd had no one, no family, because she'd completely filled the emptiness in his gut. Then when she left, he'd felt all the more alone for having known but lost her.

Sterling's straight, chestnut-colored hair had grown longer, brushing gently against her slim shoulders. He liked it. And the two years apart had worn beautifully on her fine-boned face. She looked even lovelier than he remembered. In the brief moments he'd stood next to her, he'd taken in everything: her shapely curves; her intense, blue-green eyes; her sensuously curved lips the color of a rich Merlot wine.

Ben's stomach tightened. It had to happen sooner or later, he thought to himself. Even though Sterling had left his life, it seemed inevitable that they'd run into each other sometime while working a case. He'd like to think it meant their destinies were intimately intertwined. That even though their paths might occasionally diverge and meander, they were actually headed in the same direction. She'd been emphatic at their breakup that there was no future for the two of them, he just didn't believe it. He believed in possibilities, and though in the interim he'd given Sterling her space, the hope remained strong in him that eventually, along the way they would come together again, perhaps even stronger than before.

Ben watched Sterling drive away and couldn't help himself. Was it too much to hope maybe this time it could be different?

"Ben, you've got to look at this," called one of the officers. "It looks like the PIs who just left have a connection to the deceased.

CHAPTER 2

$\mathcal{A}$ hesitant knock sounded on the interior private office door.

"Come in," Lacey called through the door.

"Where's Michelle?" Sterling glanced quizzically at her sister. "Don't tell me you gave our secretary the day off, again."

"Her cat started labor this morning," Lacey said, getting up to greet the woman who pushed the door open a crack. "Hi, Sara."

Sterling continued, amazed. "Again?"

"I thought it was a familiar excuse, but what could I say?"

"How about, no?"

"You know Michelle." Lacey winced guiltily. "She had a feeling about the labor."

"Premonition? You mean the cat wasn't even in labor?"

"It's hard to argue with Michelle's psychic feelings."

"Lacey?" The small, very polished woman in a gray suit stood uncomfortably in the doorway

"Sorry, Sara. Our secretary is off today. We didn't hear you come in," Lacey said. "Have a seat."

Sterling nodded her acknowledgment, but the woman hardly noticed.

Sara continued to stand. "You left a message on my machine saying you needed to see me right away."

"Yes. We have some news about your case."

A look of distress clouded Sara's eyes. "Is there a problem?"

Sterling motioned to a chair. "Please, won't you sit down?"

Sara stiffly lowered herself to the chair, perching rigidly on the edge as Lacey opened a drawer and pulled out photos. Sterling heard Sara draw in a sharp breath and saw panic flame in her eyes.

"Let's start at the beginning," Lacey said. "You hired us to find out if your husband, Jerry, was involved with another woman."

Sterling sat motionless, as though doing so could somehow soften the blow. This part of the job never got easier. Lacey would be gentle, but hearing the truth had to hurt, and this middle-aged woman looked quite vulnerable, sitting there fingering the strap of her purse.

"Your suspicions proved correct." Lacey's words brought no reaction. She went on. "This picture was taken of him entering her condo. And this one is of the two of them in his car. We followed them to this restaurant."

Sterling watched Sara's expressionless reaction and thought she'd seen it all. Upon officially learning of a spouse's infidelity, clients had been known to rage, cry, or even burst out laughing. But this blankness, this complete lack of emotion seemed incredibly weird.

Lacey pressed on. "We traced phone records and there is every indication that Jerry and this woman, Pamela Witt, had been engaged in an affair for months. He has a bank account you probably don't know about. Jerry has been paying the mortgage for the condo. Apparently Pamela worked as an investment counselor at the bank where your husband is vice president." Lacey eyed the woman, then reached over to take her hand. "I'm sorry, Sara."

Lacey's move to console her client might not be SOP for most professional PIs, but it was very true to her big heart, and something that Sterling admired.

Sara took in a deep breath and let it out slowly. "Well, this is not surprising," she said. "There have been clues. You know, the usual. Coming home late with heavy perfume scent on his clothes, awkward phone calls, stuff like that. Still, I wanted it to be just my imagination." Her voice trailed off like a toy whose battery had run low, and she stared at the floor.

"We understand, Sara," Sterling offered. "Can I get you a glass of water?"

"No. I'll just be going. I have to think." Sara started to rise.

Lacey glanced at Sterling and back at Sara. "I'm afraid there's more."

Sara stopped in her chair. "More?"

"Pamela is dead." Lacey's words came out gently.

Sterling noted Sara's expression barely changed.

"Dead?"

"Murdered," Sterling added.

"When? How do you know?"

"We know because we found her body this morning." Lacey walked around to perch on the top of her desk and face Sara directly. "The police think she was murdered this morning about nine o'clock, two hours before we found her."

"You found her?"

"We planned to sit surveillance at her condo but noticed her front door was open, so we went inside. We found her body in the bathtub. We won't know the actual cause of death until after we see the coroner's report."

"Have you seen Jerry today?" Sterling had to ask the obvious question.

Finally, tears began rolling down Sara's perfectly made-up face. "No. He had already left for work this morning when I got up."

"You know this doesn't look good for Jerry." Lacey offered the woman a tissue.

"What do you mean?" Sara wiped her nose and dabbed carefully at her eyes.

"It's too soon to say, but I wouldn't be surprised if the police look to him as a prime suspect once they make the connection, which they will," Lacey said.

"Why would he kill her?"

"Maybe I shouldn't have said anything." Lacey stood and motioned toward the door. "Why don't you go home. The police will handle it from here."

"I don't know what to do?" Sara stood but remained planted in the spot, the look of a lost doe on her face. "Will you find him, please?"

"Do you mean you want us to stay on the case?" Sterling asked.

"You have to. What if something terrible has happened to him? His secretary said he's out of town, but it isn't like him not to tell me. Something's wrong, I'm sure. Will you find him?" Sara pleaded.

Sterling could hardly believe her ears. This woman seemed genuinely concerned for her husband -- her cheating husband.

"Of course we will." Lacey exchanged a look with Sterling.

"Oh, thank you. I don't know what to do." Sara looked more and more lost by the second.

Sterling felt sickened by the thought that apparently even a worthless husband could provide a woman with an element of definition. Or was it a template? At any rate, Sara seemed like a ship that had just lost its mooring. The feeling echoed menacingly inside Sterling, calling up barely conscious defenses from the swamps of her soul. She moved into action.

"Just go home and do what you normally do," Sterling said, walking her out to the door and wishing she could do more to help the woman. It seemed like Sara's life was rapidly disintegrating. "Call us if you need something, okay?"

"Thank you. I will," Sara mumbled.

Sterling opened the door for Sara and let out a startled cry. Ben's tall frame and broad shoulders succinctly blocked the doorway.

"Aegar Investigations," he read from the door. "I always wondered what your office would look like, Sterling." He flashed the easy smile that used to melt her heart. "For the longest time it's been impossible for me to picture you in a private office."

Annoyed, she ignored him. "Good bye, Sara."

Sterling abruptly turned back toward her office and Ben followed close behind.

"An unhappy client?"

Sterling didn't know which she hated more, Ben's sarcasm or his disdain.

He went on. "Tell me, do you deal mostly with rejected wives or conniving mistresses? Or do you stick mainly to dull insurance fraud?"

Sterling stopped short in the outer reception area and turned to glare at him. "Are you here sightseeing, visiting a friend in the neighborhood, or are you scoping out my office because you're considering a career change?"

Ben scoffed. "I'm definitely not considering going out to pasture in some pristine office with no greater reward than collecting money from disgruntled wives."

"Don't presume to know my work. You clearly don't know anything about it." Sterling was shaking inside. "Life is good. I don't need to live on the edge like you do."

"You apparently still don't know anything about my work. I don't care what you say, we both know you'd be better off being a great detective on the force than sidelined, working second-rate, meaningless wanna-be crimes." Hardness flamed in his eyes.

His eyes, she thought to herself as she stared up into them. The deep blue eyes that could emanate such warmth. Warmth she used to bask in. The eyes that could speak as much uncensored merriment as his hearty laughter.

"What? No clever comeback?" he snapped.

Feeling a warm glow begin to creep into her cheeks, Sterling walked to the files and began sorting through some papers. If Ben could read her mind, he'd know that she lost a beat in their stupid little debate because she got caught up in his eyes. Those eyes served his profession well, she knew. Keen like a hawk's eyes, they never missed anything, so she didn't dare face him. Not right now, with her thoughts so incredibly out of control.

"That's right, just ignore me. It worked for you before."

His remark hit the center of her heart, leaving her weak. "Please," she said, still facing away, "simply state your business or get out." Sterling willed time to fly by, but instead it came to an abrupt halt. She could hear Ben shift his weight from one foot to another. Tension in the room screamed for release.

At last, Ben spoke. "Fine. I'm here to discuss the Witt murder with you and Lacey. You two found the body and you might know something helpful. I know you talked to the guys on the scene, but I have more questions. Is Lacey around here?"

"I'm sure if you open that door there," said Sterling motioning to their private office, "you'll find her pressing her ear against it."

Ben chuckled. "Some things never change."

Sterling let her shoulders relax. The sound of his laughter broke the tension, sending it skirting through the air like leaves caught up in a brisk breeze.

Sliding into her chair behind her desk, Sterling watched Ben relax into the couch in the private office. He didn't waste any time getting to the point.

"I understand you two were working a surveillance on Pamela Witt. I expect it was a standard infidelity situation, right?"

With Ben's sultry eyes aimed at her, Sterling could hardly think. Thankfully, Lacey spoke up.

"Yes, that's right. Finding the dead woman surprised us."

"Hmm." Ben looked away and rubbed his chin thoughtfully. He pulled out contents from an envelope. "We found this at the crime scene. It was inside Jerry Rutherford's coat. He must have left it there. Your agency's phone number is penned on the back of Pamela's business card. And then there's this print out of an old newspaper article." Ben spread contents of the envelope on Sterling's desk. "Do you have an explanation for why the guy and the deceased would have your agency's phone number and this clipping of your father's death in their possession?"

Lacey looked at Sterling and Sterling looked back, nerves firing throughout her body. "That is curious," she said, trying to maintain her composure. She could never have seen this coming. Her thoughts spun in a million different directions but her heart went cold. "I would like to know what's behind it, as well. Right off, I don't know."

"Well, I can understand that. But you can understand my concern about the implications."

"Ben, I don't know what you're getting at, but surely you're not implying we're somehow complicit in the murder." Sterling, still too stunned by the clipping, could hardly think.

"I'm just following the investigation."

"You don't think it's a little strange that this guy left his jacket and other belongings at the scene?"

"Yeah. I'm no cop but isn't that what you'd call a little off, circumstantial, set up?" asked Lacey.

Sterling frowned at her sister's choice of words. "If it's an answer you want, you'll have to wait. We need time to figure this out."

Silence ticked by as Ben pursed his lips and scanned the room. "I like what you've done with your office. It's nice."

"Thanks." Sterling felt surreal. *Are we really going to talk about décor?*

He unfolded his long legs and headed for the outer office. "You've got my number. Just give me a call when you've got some information."

Sterling watched Lacey walk him out to the door and tuned out the small talk. She had to avoid future confrontations with him. She would simply insist, no beg, Lacey to handle this case. Even after two years apart, too much pain flowed between her and Ben.

"Wow, that was fun," Lacey exclaimed wryly and grabbed a watering can. "I need to de-stress. Can you believe that? Where did that clipping come from? And why did Pamela or Jerry have our number? I don't' see the connection."

"Maybe that's because there isn't one."

"It's crazy-making."

Sterling absentmindedly watched Lacey water the English ivy and African violets sitting in the morning sun-splashed window of their fourth floor office in downtown Laurelwood. She knew judging by their appearances, no one would guess she and her sister shared the same genes. Unlike her own brown, straight hair, Lacey's hair was the color of burnished copper and curled naturally around her face and shoulders. While she herself stood only slightly over five feet, Lacey was a lanky five feet, seven inches. Growing up the youngest, Sterling remembered a longing to reach the same height, but at twenty-six years of age, she felt resigned to always being what Lacy fondly called her, "little" sister.

"Nice hairdo," Sterling commented. Some of Lacey's curls were pulled into a careless ponytail and secured with a wide band at the back of her head, while the rest of her hair hung loosely above her shoulders.

"I know you don't mean that." Lacey chuckled, continuing to give her plants a drink.

"Yes I do."

"I think it may look a little young, but my therapist says demonstrating my latent adolescent expression through my choice of style is perfectly normal." The smile she shot Sterling belied her insecurities.

"Well, it looks nice. So no explanation needed." Lacey's youthful style complemented her pretty face and matched the cream shirt and brown pants she was wearing –– casual but chic.

"I'm going out for coffee. Want some?" Lacey asked.

"Sure. Tall and black."

The door shutting behind Lacey let Sterling know she was alone, since Michelle hadn't yet made an appearance.

Sterling didn't know if she could bring herself to do a search on her father to see if it revealed any connection to Jerry or Pamela, nonetheless she turned her attention to her computer. But troubled feelings immediately distracted her and she let the silence soothe her as thoughts cascaded.

The therapist, the little quirks, and compulsive tendencies all pointed out that Lacey had made her way through a lot of pain. Sterling admired her sister for not giving up, as their mother had.

The calendar sitting on her desk told her it would soon be two years since Lacey's husband, Nicholas, had been killed while on duty as a policeman. An apparently simple traffic stop had turned ugly when the driver pulled out a gun and shot Nicholas. And just like her father's murderer, the shooter had disappeared. A fatal flaw in the randomness of life and a cruel fact that reverberated throughout Sterling's life.

It still scared her to think of how closely Lacey's life paralleled their mother's. Marrying a cop, becoming a mother, then becoming a widow.

Sterling felt the familiar heaviness in her chest thinking of how her mother was never the same after her dad died while on duty. Her mother began her retreat into depression the night the county corner came to the door and told them her father had been shot in the head during a drug bust and the shooter had gotten away. With a single bullet from some unknown assailant's gun, she and Lacey essentially lost both their parents. Although her mother still cared for them, the spark was gone.

Sterling's heart tightened, thinking of coming home from school and finding her mother still lying in bed or sitting on the couch, staring into space. Too overwhelmed in sorrow, her mother hadn't noticed the piles of laundry. And when the food ran out, it was Lacey who restocked the refrigerator and the cupboards. Although their father's insurance had provided for a moderate lifestyle, Sterling and her sister lived in vigilance of a late utility bill or overdrawn checking account, details that could escape their mother's attention.

Propping up her feet on her desk, Sterling leaned back into her chair and closed her eyes. The sounds of the streets below —- traffic flowing through the downtown streets, construction workers putting finishing touches on a new facade for an art theatre, and distant sirens announcing that someone was on the way to the emergency room -- played in the background like a well-known song on the radio.

Without much effort, Sterling could summon up the empty feeling that pervaded after her father's death. Although her mother would make an effort to go through the motions of many of the day-to-day needs as she could muster energy, little things were missing. There were no more impromptu trips to a sunny park to giggle under a shady tree while savoring deli sandwiches and mangos. No more afternoons at the art museum in tow of their mother, who had loved

Impressionist paintings. Only a memory remained of huddling close to her as she spoke in hushed tones about Renoir and Monet.

When everything eventually came crashing down, their mother suffered a nervous breakdown and Lacey, being the oldest, had stepped in to take over as caretaker, surrendering her youthful years. Although Sterling had never sensed Lacey begrudged her obligation, it was clear her sister had lost precious years of kicking up her heels as most teenagers and young adults do.

Sterling let her feet drop to the floor and squirmed in her seat. She had long since given up on her mother. For Sterling, the memories of the fights, of railing against her mother's willingness to "disappear," were too hard to be present with for any length of time. But the inescapable overtook her. She closed her eyes again and let her pain take her back.

"How can you just sit there?" Sterling shouted. *"I need your help with my science project. All the other parents are helping."*

"Are all the other parents alone?" her mother asked, *not moving from the couch. Her beautiful blonde hair uncombed and in disarray, fanned out like a wild-woman's mane.*

"We all lost him, Mom. We have to go on. You can't just drop out of life."

"You're so cruel, Sterling. You just don't understand what it's like. I'm trying my best."

"Well it's not good enough."

Sterling took a deep breath and slowly let it out. The disappointment, unexpressed, tightly-contained sorrow and anger clenched her fists as she said no once again to its full weight.

In time, her mother's declining health forced Sterling and her sister to face the decision of placing her in an assisted living home. Sterling closed the door to her mother, but Lacey remained by her side, insisting on top-notch care and making regular visits.

Then Nicholas stepped into her sister's life. After all the loneliness and gloom of their young years, he had been like a breath of fresh of air for Lacey. Finally, she'd been able to enjoy a full and satisfying life filled with love.

But, again, the security and love had been taken away.

When Lacey lost Nicholas to a bullet too, it seemed like a cruel joke with her family as the brunt. But losing him didn't permanently crush her sister. Lacey rallied her resources and put all of herself into nurturing her little son. Tyler had been a scant four years old when his father was killed.

Sterling smiled to herself, feeling proud of Lacey for taking classes in criminal justice and getting PI experience under Sterling's license. Launching their partnership had really been a lifesaver for both of them during some rough times. Maybe it wasn't as action packed as working on the force, but it occupied time and it paid the bills. And although Lacey remained Mrs. Nicholas Owen in her heart, she was all Aegar, going by the family name in her profession.

She tried to focus her attention back to the Rutherford case. The clipping, the business card with the agency number written on it -- it didn't make sense. It made her feel vulnerable and that was never a good space to be in. Agitation stood her to her feet and she paced the small office in controlled steps.

Looking around their comfortable office, Sterling felt comforted by how it reflected their divergent personalities. Lacey liked colorful country curtains and Sterling preferred somber blinds. Lacey enjoyed pictures of barns and frolicking children adorning the walls, while Sterling could do without anything but modern art. Still, they managed compromises and everything worked as a whole. She liked that.

The walls of their two-room office were papered in a tiny blue and white check. Country blue and white sashes picked up the same check and complemented the slate blinds on the windows. Splashes of colors and geometric shapes in a modern art painting framed in rustic wood hung on the wall. The muted colors of a wildflower arrangement softened the angles of an exotic vase. Sterling got her clean lines with a white leather sofa and Lacey got her cozy look with accent pillows covered in mauve and heather blue hydrangeas.

Lacey bustled in, the promise of delicious coffee from the coffee shop down the block leading her, interrupting Sterling's thoughts. Sterling inwardly marveled at how lost she'd become in wayward thoughts. A little bit of Ben and was easily thrown back through the past without hesitation.

"Tall. Black," Lacey announced, setting the cup on Sterling's desk. "Sorry to take so long. I got behind the cinnamon dolce latte and white chocolate mocha crowd."

"What did you get?" Sterling eyed her sister mischievously. She knew her sister enjoyed the drinks with some bells and whistles, too.

Lacey sat back in her desk chair and sipped slowly from her cup before slanting a look at Sterling. "Espresso macchiato, double shot."

Sterling nodded appreciatively, but her thoughts refocused to the case. There would be an explanation for why Pamela Witt had written the Aegar Detective Agency phone number on her business card and maybe given it to Jerry. Of course there would be an explanation, and she couldn't wait to discover it. Meanwhile, she'd had enough of ruminating and pacing. Time to get to work.

"I'm going to the bank to see what Jerry's secretary has to say." Sterling grabbed her coat and coffee and headed toward the door.

"Do you want me to come with?" Lacey titled her head in question but seemed pretty content where she sat.

"No. We don't want to seem like we're storming the castle and put the woman on the defense, but thanks. You man the fort and enjoy your coffee.

CHAPTER 3

Sterling stepped out into the spring day and breathed out a deep sigh. The bank where Jerry worked was only a few blocks away from her office. A brisk walk with the promise of a productive destination would put her thoughts where they belonged -- on the case.

Reaching the bank's heavy glass doors, Sterling swung them open, marched through and glanced around for a directory. With the office number in her head, she strode to the elevator, the sound of her heels striking the stone floor in the large lobby. She entered the elevator, pushed the button for the eighth floor and focused her thoughts. Moments later, as she stepped out of the elevator her breath caught. Ben.

"Sterling. You following me?" He gave her a lopsided grin.

"Of course not." A little unnerved, she shot him a dismissive glance as she attempted to brush past him, but his eyes pinned her gaze and slowed her steps.

"Good luck with the secretary. There's not much information there, though." His eyes gleamed disarmingly as he entered the elevator.

"Just doing my job," she tossed over her shoulder and retrained her sight on Jerry's office. When she heard the elevator door swoosh closed she dared a backward glance. Geez, stars are aligned or planets are colliding, she wondered, her shoulders tightening. Ben's inexplicable persistent appearance in her life troubled her. She didn't need the added distraction.

The young, attractive woman at the desk in Jerry's outer office flashed a composed, glossy smile at Sterling. "Can I help you?"

"I'm looking for Jerry Rutherford. Is he in?" It didn't hurt to start with the most obvious question, Sterling thought.

The woman's smile wilted a bit. "No, I'm sorry, Mr. Rutherford is out of town. Did you have an appointment? I'm sorry it wasn't rescheduled."

"When do you expect him back?"

"Umm, well, I'm not sure," she stammered. "He left unexpectedly. What did you say your name is?"

"Sterling Aegar. What's yours?" Sterling had noted the absence of a name plate when she'd approached the secretary's desk.

"Janice Martin. I'm Mr. Rutherford's secretary, and as I said, he's not here. Is there anything else I can do for you?"

The smile was still there, so Sterling pressed on. "I'm sorry to bother you but I have a few questions. I'm working on behalf of Mr. Rutherford's wife."

The young woman's eyes widened and the smile dropped. "What does that mean, you're working on behalf of Mr. Rutherford?"

"I'm a private detective. As you can understand, Mrs. Rutherford is concerned and it's her understanding that Mr. Rutherford is missing. That's all she's been told, can you believe it?"

"Poor woman."

The young woman pursed her lips in dismay. This was what Sterling had hoped for. "I'm sure it's just some kind of simple misunderstanding, but, Janice, if you could tell me when was the last time you spoke with him, I'm sure we can clear it up pretty quickly."

"I've already talked to a detective this afternoon. I'll tell you what I told him. If you want any information you'll have to talk to public relations." The woman rose abruptly and looked like she was searching for a quick and quiet escape.

"I'm sorry to trouble you, Janice. I don't want you to reveal anything that would get you in trouble." Sterling glanced over her left shoulder, her right shoulder, then leaned close. "I've heard a nasty rumor and I would like to spare Mrs. Rutherford and you and everyone else at the bank the embarrassment of it."

The woman's shoulders slumped and she sighed heavily. "It is already that. It has been such an embarrassment for some time," she said in low tones, shaking her head. "And I've kept it quiet because, well, I didn't know quite what to do. Mrs. Rutherford deserves better. Better than what Mr. Rutherford has given her."

"By that you mean the other woman?" Bait and wait seemed to be working, Sterling thought, getting slightly giddy inside.

"Of course. The two of them kept it pretty low key in the office, but it wasn't much of a secret that Mr. Rutherford was spending lunches, shall we say, with Pamela. So clichéd."

"Clichéd? How so?"

"The young ambitious bank executive and the older man. Pamela had him wrapped around her finger." The woman's voice fell to a staged whisper. "But the worst of it is the strange bookkeeping."

Sterling's heart skipped. "Really? How awful."

Her eyes darted warily, but the young woman continued. "I don't know anything about it but I overheard some executives discussing the problem with the account information in Mr. Rutherford's computer files and they're trying to keep it quiet. I'm sure you can understand. If this got out, well, it wouldn't be good for our top-tiered customers, which would be bad for us all."

"So you haven't had a chance to talk with Mr. Rutherford today?"

The young woman bit her lip nervously. "He left me a voicemail this morning. He said he had a business trip to Chicago and he would be in touch later. That's all I know. Although there is some rumor that his lady friend is missing too, so maybe they ran off together. I hate to speculate."

Sterling believed the woman didn't know anything more. She

wasn't sure Janice even knew that Pamela had been murdered. Apparently the bank's executives hadn't had time or concern enough to give all the employees the news. Hopefully they'd be told about the death before they heard it on the evening news."Well, you've been very helpful, Janice, and I appreciate your concern about discretion." Sterling handed her a business card and smiled. "If you have anything you'd like to talk about, please don't hesitate to call me or stop by my office."

Janice nodded and sat back down, letting her attention fall to her paperwork on her desk.

On her way back to her office Sterling called her sister to let her know what she'd learned about Jerry but the answering machine picked up. She glanced at the time and realized Lacey would have left to be home when her son got off school. It wouldn't hurt for her to take off early herself, Sterling thought. She had files at home she could work on, but a good run before the day ended would help settle the nerves rattled by her day. She didn't even bother to go upstairs to her office when she reached the parking lot and her car. With all that had happened, Sterling felt that she was struggling to stay present in one place.

She climbed in behind the wheel and leaned back against the seat. Emotions stirred inside her heart and she closed her eyes to focus her breath. Strength ebbed and Sterling couldn't muster the will to hold back the memories that always sat just outside of view, demanding attention she refused to give. In the quiet and growing darkness, Sterling gave up the struggle and was back there again, the day she said good bye to her dad.

She'd stood in a slight drizzle crying around her and the crisp air. The cold dampness and the bleakness of it all seemed appropriate to her at twelve years old. Cold and bleak. That's how she felt. She stood under the tent with her mother and older sister, Lacey, staring at her father's casket, and struggled with her impulse to scream out in protest. *This is all wrong.* Her father coached her softball team, ran in marathons and loved to dance. He couldn't be cold and silent.

Her mother's sobs pierced the memories raging inside Sterling's head, and again she faced the stark reality -- *Dad is gone.*

Sterling thought of the night the shift sergeant and county coroner sat in her living room explaining how her dad, Joshua Aegar, had gotten shot during a drug bust.

"Your husband was taken by surprise, Mrs. Aegar. He was conducting a routine procedure. Unfortunately, someone must have been tipped-off and was waiting for him. He was wearing a protective vest, but the shot went to his head. There was nothing we could do. I'm very sorry for your loss."

That explained how her dad died. It didn't settle the big question looming so large in her mind it was all she could think of -- *why?* There was no just and fair reason to explain why her father's life had been taken.

Like she was there in in that terrible moment, she felt the numbness that had seeped through her as she watched the casket lower into the ground and her mother insisted they leave. But she couldn't leave when it felt so wrong, so final. She'd lingered a moment alone, remembering the way her father often told her goodnight. And she'd placed a kiss on her fingertips and tossed it into the wind. "Dad, I'll love you always."

Tears streamed down Sterling's cheeks as the memories cycled through her. She felt exhaustion take over and she grabbed for the anger that always saved her from the depths -- unless she lost control, she thought, and angrily brushed away her tears. She turned the key in the ignition and directed her attention to getting home. A good run and a hot shower would do her wonders, she told herself.

AFTER AN EVENING of playing games with Tyler and reading bedtime stories, Lacey stood at the kitchen sink, dreading the long hours of the night ahead.

It seemed no matter how she filled her evenings -- sitcom drivel, miles on the treadmill, hot chamomile tea -- she always ended up staring into the darkness. Sleep would not grant her release from the terrible aloneness that lay like pale, cold frost on her heart.

Lacey finished washing the dishes, switched off the kitchen light, and headed back to Tyler's bedroom.

A gentle glow shining from a nightlight warmed the darkness and lit her son's sleeping face as Lacey placed a kiss on his cheek and snugged up the blankets. Even at six, her son was the spitting image of his father, Lacey thought, a melancholy cord striking in her heart. Sounds of the spring evening swirled with Tyler's soft breathing and rose as prayer to Lacey's ears.

Nearly two years had passed and still Tyler's grief over his father's death conjured up all too frequent nightmares calling for Lacey's soothing in the night.

It's not fair he should suffer so. It's not fair that my son's foundation, his father and idol, should be taken away as though it means nothing.

Lacey lingered in the doorway. Unbidden, memories broke through her carefully constructed barriers. Memories of her husband wrestling with Tyler on the living room floor and her son's delight in tumbling with his dad. A father's instructions to his son on how to bounce a ball, pump his legs in the swing.

Once open, the secret, guarded place gushed one memory after another. Nicholas cheering Tyler as he took his first triumphant few pedals of a solo bike ride on his tiny new two-wheeler. Nicholas feigning capture in a game of backyard tag.

It was no wonder Tyler's sleep was disturbed, Lacey thought, directing her mind to clamp down. He'd lost too much.

But right now she was grateful Tyler looked peaceful, and she tiptoed out, quietly closing the bedroom door and padding into her room.

The clock on the mantle in the living room struck twelve midnight, echoing hollowly down the hall. If only sleep would come easy for once, she thought, as she climbed into the left side of the bed and pulled up the blankets. Two years and still she couldn't remove Nick's pillow, her only comfort from the empty spot beside her where he used to lie.

"Two years tomorrow, Nicholas, since you went away," Lacey

breathed out loud, as if somehow he could hear her. "I miss you so, Nick."

The scent of apple blossoms began to swirl hypnotically inside her head. It caught her breath as her whole body recognized the fragrance of Nick's favorite flower. Without thought, she eased into it, allowing the idea of Nicholas to take shape for just a moment.

But it's not real.

Lacey closed her eyes to the stinging tears, thoughts of Nicholas winding their way up from her heart and swathing her in a cloud of deep blue, timeless peace.

"I miss you too, honey. Go to sleep, Lacey. I'm here now.

CHAPTER 4

$\mathcal{I}$t's no use, Sterling fumed. Her brain refused to work. She sorted through the case files at her office, willing her emotions to stop tormenting her as she recuperated from a long sleepless night. The benign sounds of Michelle keyboarding in the outer office did little to interrupt the mindless emotional turmoil of last night's restlessness.

In the darkness, thoughts of Ben and how it used to be, what she'd done to him, replayed unrestricted by the distractions of daylight. Against her will, the memories and self-accusations surfaced, and along with them the angst and sorrow cut her like shards of jagged glass.

In the light of day, the thoughts, haughty and determined, challenged her sanity, coaxing her to give them room to do their work. But Sterling squared off and sent them back where they belonged, buried deep. In the light of day she could muster her strength of purpose and direct her thoughts toward puzzling out the case at hand -- finding Sara's husband and giving the woman a chance at reclaiming her own life.

Or at least she tried.

It troubled her that the warning flags were up again. What were they trying to say? Were they warning her of a big problem with the case? Or were they trying to tell her to beware of involvement with Ben? It could lead to more pain, and she knew it.

Two years ago she'd told him it was over. Loving him had been so easy, but then the fear welled too greatly inside of her. With Nicholas's death, she'd realized more than ever that a heart open to love was also a heart vulnerable to excruciating pain and insurmountable loss.

Silly girl. You'd actually believed in a happily-ever-after.

The break-up had been difficult, but she'd only done what she needed to survive. And even when Ben finally accepted that they weren't going to be together, endorsing her decision to quit police work was quite another matter, something he railed against with all his usual unrestrained gusto.

But Sterling knew in time she'd get over Ben. And fortunately she didn't need his permission to make a life as a private investigator. He didn't even have to like it.

To make sure no one would get close enough to leave her hurt and broken like her mother, she'd made a life for herself invested in independence. Lacey liked to point out that Sterling's single-minded devotion to her profession was her own way of building walls against the world. Maybe so, Sterling mused. Maybe no one would get in. Especially not Ben Kirby. It didn't have to make sense to be right for her.

Sterling dropped her forehead into the heels of her hands. If only life hadn't cruelly smashed them up against each other again. If only Ben would stop forcing her into a corner where she questioned her decisions.

Lacey strode in, the aroma of fresh baked cinnamon rolls wafting in with her. "Have you had breakfast yet, sis? I gave Michelle a roll and there's plenty for you, too."

Sterling's stomach lurched. "Sorry. The rolls smell delicious, but my stomach isn't ready for food yet."

Lacey eyed her. "Is something up?"

"You tell me. You seem very chipper this morning."

"I actually slept last night. Umm, there's nothing like a good night's sleep," Lacey cooed. "But stop changing the topic. What's wrong with your stomach?"

"Nothing. Michelle made coffee. It's pretty good."

"Stop trying to change the topic."

Savoring a sip from her coffee cup, Sterling quizzically watched Lacey cut her roll into bite size pieces. A new quirk?

"What?" Lacey asked defensively. "It's neater this way. Just watch. Soon everyone will be eating cinnamon rolls this way."

"I'm for whatever makes you happy, sis. In fact, I bought you something that might make you smile." Sterling pulled a pair of rose quartz earrings from a bag under her desk and walked to Lacey's desk.

"For me?" Lacey's eyes brightened as she accepted the dangling earrings.

"For you."

"What's the occasion?"

"Nothing special. When I saw them they had your name written all over them." According to the jeweler, the rose quartz stones bestow powers of love for the holder. Sterling didn't believe in all that mystical, magical stuff, but Lacey did, and it wouldn't hurt to give her a little extra love right now.

If the truth were known, Sterling would have to admit, though she worried about Lacey, she admired her buoyant spirit and anything she could do to support her recovery from losing Nicholas was worth doing. On this second anniversary of his death, Sterling couldn't bring Nicholas back, but she could at least show her sister how much she cared.

"I love them!" Lacey exclaimed, giving Sterling a quick hug. "Now let's get back to what's eating you. I can tell something's on your mind."

Sterling cleared her throat uncomfortably. "I need to talk to you about this Witt case."

"Talk away."

"I want you to handle the case alone."

"Okay. Now I understand," Lacey mumbled through cinnamon roll. She gave Sterling a once over.

"Don't give me that look," said Sterling, dropping into her desk chair.

Lacey's eyes widened innocently. "What look?"

"That knowing look that says you think I'm still hung up on Ben. The look that says you think I should settle things with him once and for all, not run away."

"My look said all that?"

Sterling nodded her head at her sister. "Trust me. I know that look."

"Sterling, I think you should live your life your way." Lacey licked cinnamon from her fork, then swallowed a mouthful of coffee.

"That's it? That's all you want to say?" Sterling knew her sister all too well. Lacey always bubbled with thoughts and was never shy about sharing them.

"Well, I think you two are perfect for each other. I think you're kidding yourself if you believe work alone will fulfill you. I think--"

Both Sterling and Lacey jumped at the sound of the intercom.

"There is a Detective Kirby to see you both," Michelle said. "Shall I send him in?"

In a whisper, Sterling pressed Lacey. "So you'll handle it alone?"

"Sure. Michelle, send him in."

Lacey walked to the door and greeted him. "Come in please."

Ben strode through the doorway into the office and Sterling's heart instantly leaped into her throat. Damn him, she thought to herself while offering a perfunctory smile. *Why does he affect me so?* A crisp white shirt set off his dark good looks. His gray suit a perfect fit, flattered his strongly muscled body. It was all heady stuff that worked at her already jangled nerves.

"Good morning, Lacey, Sterling." Ben nodded in Sterling's direction.

"Have a seat, Ben." Lacey motioned to the couch. "What brings you to our neighborhood again?"

"I have more questions regarding the Pamela Witt murder." Ben settled into the couch, all the while eyeing Sterling.

"I told you everything yesterday," Lacey said.

"Did you find out the information I asked about?"

"As soon as we have something for you we'll let you know. You haven't given us much time to work on it, Ben," Lacey added.

Fully aware of his eyes on her, Sterling gathered her purse and jacket from her desk, wanting to bound out faster than a jack rabbit. "Ben, Lacey will be working alone on this case, so if you'll excuse me, I'll leave you two alone."

Ben's eyes narrowed and Sterling felt as though he could see right into her head.

It had always been like that with him. From the moment they'd first met, they'd finished each other's sentences and anticipated each other's actions. Her face felt warm and her skin dimpled annoyingly.

"I suppose the next thing you'll say is there is nothing personal intended." His tone was as crisp as burnt toast.

"I wouldn't try to sell that to you, Ben." She saw him angrily ball his hands. This wasn't going very well. "I think you know as well as I do, we can't work in the same room, much less cooperate on a case." It was funny how the passion that used to burn so hot between them, illuminating a bigger-than-life love, now boiled beneath the surface like an angry pot threatening to erupt.

"So, as usual, you're going to walk out."

"Okay, okay, time out," Lacey interrupted, pounding her hand against her desk. "Ben, our agency wishes to cooperate with the investigation, but Sterling's direct involvement with the case has ended. Besides, I know as much as she does and I saw everything she saw. Don't sweat it."

Ben knitted his brow, and drew in a deep breath. Still staring at Sterling, he exhaled heavily. "Okay, I'm sorry for acting like such a jerk."

"Now, what do you want to know?" Lacey leaned back in her chair, ready to talk.

Sterling quietly shoved her arms into her jacket, thinking how lucky she was to have such a great sister. As she walked to the door, she made a mental note to buy Lacey some double chocolate pecan ice cream -- her favorite.

The phone intercom buzzed and Sterling quickly picked up the receiver. Michelle told her the Laurelwood Elementary school nurse was on the phone for Lacey.

As Sterling stood waiting in the awkward silence hanging between her and Ben, she read the look on Lacey's face.

Lacey replaced the receiver and Sterling's heart flinched as she watched the color drain from her sister's face. "What's wrong?"

"Tyler fell off the swing set at school. They're taking him to the hospital."

The frozen look on Lacey's face gripped Sterling hard. Her sister had already suffered too much. Her son meant everything to her. "Do you want me to go with you?" Sterling grabbed Lacey's coat and offered it to her.

Lacey mechanically pulled on her coat and smiled. "I'm sure it's nothing. You know how schools are. They're over-reacting. Tyler is always getting scuffed up. I'll call you." Pausing on her way out the door, she added, "I'm sorry, Sterling. I guess you'll have to talk over the case with Ben."

Sterling waved dismissively. "Don't worry about it, Lacey. Just go and take care of my nephew."

Sterling tossed her jacket on a nearby chair, keenly aware of the tension filling the space inside the four walls.

Ben thoughtfully rubbed his chin. "I guess you're stuck with me, babe."

Sterling gritted her teeth. He knew she hated being called "babe" -- it sounded so dismissive -- but she would not grant him the satisfaction of an angry reaction. Drawing up her composure, she calmly slid into her chair and faced Ben. "What do you want to know?"

Ben shifted in his seat. "What is your relationship with Sara Rutherford?"

"She's a client. You know that."

"Do you know the whereabouts of her husband, Jerry Rutherford?"

"No, I'm not working on the case." Sterling felt like she was sitting under an interrogator's hot lights. Ben knew how to put on the pressure. On top of that, there was so much un-named electricity arcing between them it felt like they could combust.

Ben shifted in his seat and Sterling got a whiff of his cologne. The spicy fragrance brought up so many memories and the very feelings she did not want to feel. She cleared her throat and waited for Ben to continue.

"Do you know where Mrs. Rutherford was at nine a.m. yesterday morning?" he asked, leaning forward.

"No. What are you getting at?"

"I'm merely covering all aspects of the investigation. Have you forgotten the basic rules of investigation?"

Sterling was on her feet. Hands planted on her hips, she stared him down. "Don't patronize me. Why do I get the feeling Sara is a suspect?"

Ben leaned back against the couch. "I'll ask the questions," he said, setting his jaw. "Did Sara know about the mistress?"

"Are you suggesting Sara is a murder suspect? You're joking, right?"

"I'm not suggesting anything."

"I can read between the lines. What kind of evidence do you have?" Sterling strode in front of her desk to stand directly in front him. Ben seemed calm, in control. It made her insides squirm.

"I never said Sara is a suspect."

"So she's not a suspect?"

Standing to his feet, Ben looked down at her with those eyes and sent chills running through her. His look was cold, shielded.

"Can we get back to where I ask the questions?"

Sterling swallowed hard and turned away. "Strong-arming me isn't going to get you anywhere. Besides, I have other appointments." She turned back to face him. *Why do we have to come at each other with our fists raised?*

Ben shrugged. "Have it your way. Maybe we better stop right here, but you know I'll be back."

"I'm sure you can find your way out." With the sense of him nearly overpowering her, Sterling busied herself with papers.

Silently, Ben walked to the door. Sterling couldn't stop herself. She turned to watch him and then it was too late. She couldn't pull her eyes from his strong frame. Even dressed in his conservative suit, he exuded untamed masculinity. His thick, dark hair shone like a luxurious mane. His strong shoulders, his sure stride -- all declarations of his wild spirit.

He paused at the door without turning around. "Please tell Lacey I hope her son is okay." Leaving the door ajar, he was gone.

Sterling quickly stepped to the door and soundly shut it. Straightening her shoulders and releasing a quick breath, she thought, if only she could so easily shut him out of her thoughts.

A mixture of emotions churned inside her stomach. A case always grabbed her attention, calling up her curious and competitive nature. It was like a challenger throwing down a gauntlet. And she was gleeful to pick it up. To follow the thread of information and prove her acumen.

Yet she knew this particular case could slam her right up against the strength of powerful feelings. The very feelings that would lead to enormous pain. *The sooner this case is closed, the sooner I'll be done with Ben. He's already proving detrimental to my sanity.*

Still, she couldn't shut out the small voice inside her head that questioned, would she ever truly be done with Ben?

BEN WIPED the sweat out of his eyes with the back of his hand and reached up again for the bar. Bench-pressing his usual two hundred and fifty pounds, he gritted his teeth and willed his mind to focus on the fifth repetition.

Thoughts of Sterling had been working his mind, stirring up emotions, ever since the moment he'd walked up to her at the Witt murder scene. It didn't help that this morning when he dropped by the Aegar Investigations office, Sterling had looked flawless, perfect. Her red suit was the picture of professionalism, but it couldn't hide her gentle curves. And he could never forget the exquisite joy of running his hands along those sweetly feminine curves.

"Okay, let's add another twenty pounds, Chris," Ben said, sitting up and reaching for another weight. He chided himself. *It's the past, man, forget it.*

"What are you training for, the Olympics?" his spotter asked, adding on another steel weight to match the one Ben added.

Lying back down on the weight bench, Ben ignored his spotter's question. *Best if no one knows what's eating me up.* He reached up and put everything he had into hoisting the barbell over his head. Memories of peering deeply into the wells of Sterling's eyes, dusky with passion, grabbed hold of his gut. The two of them had always connected in such a way that intimacy went beyond the physical realm. It bordered on the spiritual.

Well, that didn't work. Now I sound like some gushy nut job. Ben finished the last rep. and sat up to straddle the bench. "That's it for me, Chris. Want me to spot you now?"

"No. Thanks, Ben, but I'm done for the day. See ya later."

Ben lumbered to the locker room. Stripping off his shorts and muscle shirt, he walked to the shower and plunged his head into the hard spray. *Maybe I can wash her out.*

Hadn't he tried to pull his life together after she left him? It had been damn hard and it had taken the better part of the two years, but he'd thought she was finally out. Or at least as far out of his system as he could ever hope Sterling could be.

Clearly, nothing had changed with her. Sterling wanted no part of him. Ben closed his eyes and leaned weakly against the shower wall. It still hurt. No wonder running into her messed him up so easily, he thought. A gaping hole still bled inside him where she belonged.

"YOUR SON IS GOING to be fine. He needs some rest and we want to observe him over night, but I expect him to be up and around in no time." The doctor gave Lacey an assuring look and winked at Tyler, before stepping into the hallway.

Lacey heard what the doctor told her. Her son's fall from the swing had left him with a broken arm and a nasty knot on his head, along with a concussion. The doctor set Tyler's arm in a cast and prescribed bed rest and overnight observation. He'd assured her Tyler would suffer no permanent damage. Still, standing over him while he quietly watched television, Lacey remained coiled for the worst. Fears scrambled inside her like static in a thunderstorm. Life seemed so fragile, right now, and the hospital so fraught with loss. Her loss.

Catching herself mindlessly tracing an obsessive pattern on the back of her hand, Lacey wrestled down the sorrow and stretched out her limbs.

But Tyler was fine, or least fine enough for now. She would not lose her precious son.

"Aren't you going to eat your pudding, Tyler? It's chocolate, your favorite?" she tried brightly. "Does your arm hurt much or your head?"

"Not too bad." Tyler flipped through the television channels, barely noticing the programming. "Why can't I go home? I'm bored."

"You took a bad fall, sweetie." Amazed at his youthful resiliency, Lacey smiled at her son. His restlessness was a good sign. "You lost consciousness. The doctor wants to make sure you're going to be all right."

"Lost consciousness?"

"Got knocked out. Your brain went to sleep unexpectedly." The right words weren't coming, but Tyler's curiosity seemed satisfied.

Lacey wondered if Tyler had any memory of his last visit to the hospital. It was the last time he saw his father. But he was only four then, and what can a four-year-old grasp of such finality, she wondered, feeling the strength of her pain breach her defenses.

"I'm going to get a cup of coffee, honey. I'll be right back, okay?" Lacey patted her son's shoulder, her hand ice cold.

"Sure, Mom."

Heading toward the snack and beverage machines in the waiting room, Lacey's feet seemed to be moving in slow motion. Staring down, she saw them move one in front of the other, but she was watching, not feeling.

The hospital halls bustled with nurses and doctors. People passing her raised their eyes to meet hers but she quickly looked away. The strength to be present was ebbing away. She couldn't escape the memories that beckoned from every corner, even in this section of the hospital where brightly colored murals decorated the walls to cheer sick children. Memories of such tremendous heartache echoed in these halls, begging to bring Lacey to her knees.

Lacey walked past the vending machines and followed the hall to an alcove where she could isolate herself. Alone, she hoped to bite back the memories. She had to. It wouldn't do to fall apart when Tyler needed her. She had to focus on helping him get better.

Tears stung her eyes, her heart wincing as she thought of her little son's fearsome spirit. He tried to be such the little man, but she could tell he was hurting. And here she was, failing under the weight of her memories.

Lacey sank into a plush chair and rested her head in her trembling hands. *Oh God, I don't know if I can do this. I miss Nicholas so much. I need him. I want him.*

"I'm here, baby. Talk to me."

Lacey's head jerked to attention. She glanced cautiously around her left shoulder and then her right. I'm hallucinating, she thought, not knowing quite what to do.

Shaking her head and clearing her throat, Lacey wondered if she'd been pleading out loud to God and someone seized the opportunity to play a cruel joke on her. She stood up and stuck her head around the corner, searching for a prankster.

But there was no one. She stood alone with her sorrow in the alcove at the end of the hall.

I am definitely losing it, she thought, and headed back to Tyler's room.

. . .

"NICE NEIGHBORHOOD." Sterling drove along the quiet streets, in her mind standing back to observe all the clues presenting themselves.

The homes looked typical upper middle class, sporting plush green lawns and top-notch landscaping. Not palaces, but definitely homes expressing lives of comfort and affluence.

Pulling her silver sports car to a stop in front of Sara's home, Sterling sat a moment and pulled focus. Jerry Rutherford, bank vice president, husband. Born in February of 1962, he was a comfortable forty-something and so was his wife. They'd met at a party a few years after Sara graduated from the local university. The couple had no children. They'd celebrated their twenty-second wedding anniversary this year. No parties, just a quiet night at home. They kept to themselves most of the time, according to Sara.

Sterling walked to the front door and pressed the doorbell. Moments later the door opened.

"Hello, Sterling. You're right on time," Sara greeted her, leading her down a short hallway and into a pleasant-looking living room. "Have a seat."

"I know this is a difficult time for you, Sara," Sterling started. "You probably feel like your life is turning upside down."

Sara smiled thinly. "Thanks, you're very kind. Would you like something to drink? Tea or coffee?"

"Coffee would be nice if you have it." Sterling didn't really want any, but it would get Sara out of the room.

"Sure, I'll be just a second. I have some already brewing."

With Sara gone, Sterling helped herself. An anniversary clock sitting on an antique cherry desk ticked out the time. A small, framed picture of Jerry receiving some kind of banking award sat next to the clock. Sterling peered close. Jerry's eyes seemed dull, disinterested. Glancing furtively toward the doorway, Sterling pulled open the top drawer and quickly sorted through its contents. Her attention stopped as she ran her hand along the underside of the desktop. What's this, she wondered, ripping something taped there from its hiding place. *A strange looking key. How clichéd. Let me guess -- this key will open a secret safety deposit box.*

Sara's footsteps coming close warned her. Sterling shoved the key into her suit pocket and took her seat in the overstuffed chair.

"Here we go." Setting a steaming mug on a coaster on the table in front of Sterling, Sara sat back into the couch and sighed.

Sterling eyed the woman for a second, trying to get a feel for her state of mind, deciding quickly to proceed. *I need information and there's little point in stalling or making nice.* "I know you're probably wondering why I wanted to talk with you, so I'll get right to it. Have you been contacted by your husband since yesterday morning?"

"No, not all," Sara said softly, spooning sugar into her coffee.

"I'm sure the police have already spoken with you."

"I have been questioned. They asked me the same thing, but I had to tell them no. That's the truth, Sterling."

"I believe you. But I wonder if you've been contacted without knowing it." Sterling glanced around the room, then landed her gaze on Sara again.

"What do you mean?" Sara looked genuinely perplexed.

"Have you gotten any phone calls with no one on the other end? Have you come home from shopping to find things different than when you left? Anything like that?"

Sara thought for a minute. "No. Nothing like that."

"When was the last time you talked with Jerry?" Sterling knew all she had to do was be persistent and patient.

Sara's eyes seemed mesmerized by the beige sculpted carpeting. "Talked? That's a funny way to put it. The night before last. He came home late. I was already in bed, reading. He got into bed, rolled over, and said good night. That was all. No talking, really."

For the first time since she'd met her, Sterling saw emotion spark in Sara's eyes. "I see." Her instincts proved right. She suspected if she left space for the women, she would lay out the truth. Experience told her Sara didn't need much prodding, not even directing. Just space and a willing ear. "Was that normal for the two of you?"

"Jerry has never been a big conversationalist. It's funny, too, because when we met he was so charming, so gregarious. I was kind of reserved. I guess you could say he swept me off my feet. My father called Jerry a hustler, but I argued he was just free spirited. I was young and it impressed me that my father and his status didn't intimidate Jerry. I felt like I had a chance to break away. That was an illusion, youthful innocence." Sara's tone was matter-of-fact, as though she'd just reported that it was raining.

Sterling sat in silent witness to Sara's sorrow and disenchantment, amazed that the woman's composure remained solid. Apparently oppressed by her father and essentially abandoned as a young bride by her gold-digging husband, the woman deserved a break.

Sara drew up a deep breath and continued. "Life carries on. Anyway, in the last few months he's seemed even quieter, sort of pulled inside of himself. Now I know why," she said, frowning and fidgeting with a piece of lint from her shirt. "It was her."

"What about his activities? How does he spend his time?" Sterling pressed on, but took note of the angry growl in Sara's voice and emphasis on "her."

Sara walked to the desk across the room and opened the top drawer, while Sterling squirmed in her seat and fingered the key in her pocket. She had to admit, it wasn't exactly kosher to lift a piece of personal property, but yes, she sometimes bent the rules.

"This is Jerry's daily planner. He lives by it religiously, so this might help." Her hands shaking, Sara handed the small leather-bound book to Sterling. "It's odd he didn't take it with him. I didn't give it to the police and I probably should have."

"Don't worry about it. It might be nothing, but thanks." Sara seemed near the edge of breaking down. *This is all a bit much for the poor woman.* Sterling stood and walked toward the doorway out. "I'll look this over, but you be sure and call me if your husband contacts you."

Sara stopped at the front door and aimed darkly clouded eyes at Sterling. "Our marriage was one of convenience for Jerry. I've known for a long time he married me because of my father's wealth. But I loved him."

"Loved him, past tense?"

"I loved him when we got married and I have remained committed to our marriage, even though it's been pretty lifeless for a long time." Breathing a heavy sigh, she continued. "If Pamela Witt hadn't coaxed him to wander, maybe I would have had a chance. I would think twenty-two years of marriage would account for something, but I guess not." Her gaze shifted and she opened the door. "Thanks for helping, Sterling."

Stepping out into the warm afternoon, Sterling felt the oppressiveness of the house lift. "Oh, one more question," she said, turning back. "Do you or Jerry have family in this area where he could be staying?"

"No. Jerry was an only child, his parents are both dead, and my family is in Denver, Colorado. He would never go to them."

"Okay, I understand. It was just a thought."

"I know I must seem pretty pathetic to you. I have nothing, no children, no love."

"You have a lovely home, Sara, and I'm sure there must have been some love between the two of you."

A tear slipped down Sara's cheek. "I always thought there would be more. Eventually. I never gave up." Her look hardened. "Not even when I suspected another woman. That woman."

Sterling placed a hand gently to Sara's arm. "It's not too late."

"I don't know."

"I'll find Jerry, and when I do, you'll learn the truth about a lot of things. Then you'll know what to do."

"Do you think so?"

"Truth can be a hard thing, but it will always offer direction."

"Thank you, Sterling."

Walking to her car, Sterling sensed a presence, like someone reading the newspaper over her shoulder. She glanced around, but saw no one. Nearby, a dog barked insistently and tree limbs danced in the soft breeze, but nothing stood out to explain the odd feeling. If it was something she needed to pay attention to, Sterling knew it would reveal itself eventually. That's what she'd come to understand about her gut feelings, a PI's best friend.

Pulling away in her car, Sterling lit out, wanting to distance herself not only from the sense of foreboding, but from the Rutherford house.

The picture Sara had painted of her married life left Sterling with a pallid winter feeling chilling her heart. It wasn't supposed to be like that. Marriage shouldn't leave you feeling lonely, she thought. Love might just be the world's biggest joke.

It hadn't been like that for her parents, though. From back when she was very young, Sterling remembered the gleam that lit up in her mother's eyes when her dad walked in the house after a day of work, and the matching shine in her father's face. She remembered the comfortable feeling that filled her just watching her dad cuddle up to her mother. Her mom would respond by resting her head against his shoulder and Sterling had believed all was well with the world.

Tightening her grip on the steering wheel, she hardened herself to the pain cinching her breath. She'd been so naïve, so gullible. In its sweet simplicity, that life had lulled her into believing in the happily-ever-after.

All that love and security vanished, like a shimmering mirage, the night her dad died, and nothing, not even the strength of love, had been enough to shield her mother from the terrible pain.

That's the double-sided edge of love, Sterling raged to herself. *That's the joke.*

CHAPTER 5

Ben slid onto a stool at the bar, welcoming the comfort of familiar sounds of the neighborhood pub. From the tinkling of ice in glasses to the chatter and background of sports commentary on the TV hanging on the wall behind the bar, the sounds distracted his thoughts.

"What's your pleasure, tonight, Ben? A burger or just a beer?"

"Just coffee, Bridget," Ben told the bartender. He knew the hunger gnawing inside his belly couldn't be filled with a greasy hamburger. And it was not his style to dowse it with alcohol.

"Hey don't listen to him, Bridget. Give that guy a beer."

The voice came from behind him in the corner of the dimly lit room, but Ben knew who it was before he turned around. "Hi, Jay."

"Bring yourself over here and keep me company."

Ben grabbed his cup of coffee and headed to the table.

"Funny, I haven't seen you around for a while. What you been up to, old buddy?"

Jay slurred the words just enough to clue Ben that he'd been at the bar a while. Thoughtfully, he slid into a chair across the table. "Oh you know, same old same old."

"No, I don't know. Like I said, I don't see you much anymore. Not since this." Jay pointed to the cane leaning against the wall. "You're not letting this little thing keep you away, are you, buddy?"

"Of course not, Jay. I've just been working. Besides, I saw you a couple weeks ago. Here in fact." Ben held a mouthful of coffee inside his mouth, focusing on its deliciously bitter flavor before swallowing.

"Yeah, I'm here a lot these days."

Ben flinched inside. "Jay—"

"Oh I don't mean anything by that, Ben. You don't think I'm feeling sorry for myself, do you?"

"I don't know. Are you?" Ben was beginning to wish he'd never walked through the bar door tonight. It was hard to watch his friend's life take the turn it seemed to be taking.

"No. I mean, what do I have to feel sorry about?" Jay threw back another swallow of beer. "Lots of guys would love to be in my spot. Life of leisure is where it's at. Of course, not for you. You're different, right? Nose to the grindstone and all."

"Yeah. That's me." Ben eyed Jay, trying to find the person he knew. "What do you want me to say, Jay? Do you want to talk about it? If you do, then let's do it."

Jay narrowed his eyes and sat starring at his empty glass as the seconds turned to a full minute. "No. I don't want to talk about anything. I don't want to talk about the filing I do. Although it's fascinating stuff, I tell ya. I bet you didn't know that the department has a very complex filing system. It takes a really good cop to manage it."

Ben's stomach twisted harshly. He wanted to do the right thing, but damn it was so hard to know what the right thing might be. He listened to Jay go on.

"And I don't want to talk about the work behind the microphone at dispatch. That's something every cop dreams of doing. Sitting at that desk sending out calls for other cops to answer."

"Jay—"

"No, I don't want to talk about my exciting life. But you could buy me a beer, old buddy. You don't mind if I call you buddy, do you? I can't call you partner anymore."

Ben took his time with his coffee, avoiding Jay's request.

But Jay was persistent, if not sober. He leaned low over the table and clanked his empty glass on the worn wood. "I said you could buy me a beer. Then you can tell me all about your investigations. We can compare notes, just like the good old days. That'd be a hoot, don't you think?" Jay slipped back against the wall and leered at Ben.

"No. I don't think it's funny stuff, Jay. Like I said, if you want to talk, let's talk about the elephant in the room. But not when you're like this. And I won't buy you a drink, unless it's coffee."

"Oh, fine, fine." Jay shook his head. "That's my buddy Ben, always got …my…back."

The twist in Ben's stomach tightened and he just looked at Jay, unable to form words that would make any difference. "Let me take you home?"

Jay lifted his empty glass and hollered. "Bridget, baby, bring me another tall one. And somebody put on some music. My buddy here is not funny. He's putting a real chill on the mood. But he's just leaving."

Ben drew out the money from his wallet to pay his bill and walked to the cash register. Reluctance laid heavy in him. He didn't want to leave Jay alone but he felt helpless to stop the spiral. He shoved open the door and stepped out into the night. How did things get so out of control?

STERLING STOOD at her office window, staring out toward the night sky. Lights from the city twinkled like stars.

Across town, Lacey would be sitting with Tyler at the hospital. A phone call earlier from her sister had brought her up to date. Tyler, being the fearless little boy that he was, had pumped his swing so high it tipped backwards. In his excitement, he'd lost his grip and plummeted to the ground. When a teacher couldn't rouse him, the school called an ambulance to take him the hospital.

Lacey had always been a doting mother, but after her husband's death, Tyler had somehow become even more precious to her, as impossible as that could seem. But it made sense to Sterling. Tyler was indeed wonderful. More than that, he was Lacey's link with Nicholas.

Sterling knew it would take more than a two-ton truck to get Lacey very far from Tyler's side while he recuperated in the hospital. The case with Sara and Jerry would be her own responsibility after all. What had been a standard marital surveillance had turned into what should be a simple enough locate. If Ben weren't part of the picture, the case would be slam dunk for Sterling all by herself. No need for Lacey's help.

Still, something about Sara, or what was known about Jerry, did not ring true. Sterling couldn't put her finger on it, but the gut feeling stirring her insides insisted things were not as they appeared.

Why would two people stay in such a loveless relationship, she wondered. If, as Sara feared, her husband felt no love for her, why did he stick around? If love was supposed to be all it was cracked up to be, why not abandon the dead relationship and find the real thing?

Tapping her fingers against the window frame, the question prompted thoughts of another time. Sterling recalled racing the wind on the back of Ben's motorcycle and surfing the waves off the coast of California. She and Ben had ridden life as though it was a never-ending roller coaster, with one thrill following another. And at the core of it all had been love. The kind of love that gripped a heart and would never let go, never let up.

Her heart knotted as memories of a warm, summer day filled her. With packs slung on their backs, she and Ben had hiked up a steep wilderness hill during a weekend get-away. Along the way they'd paused to sit without talking while the wind brushed their faces and the sounds of nature surrounded them. From the piercing screeches of a nearby hawk, the melodic burbling of water tumbling over rocks in a sparkling stream, to craggy earthiness of rock walls jutting out from the grassy hillside, the elements of the environment heightened the thrill of being alive. Her heart beat with more vigor; her breath flowed in and out of her lungs with more fullness; and when Ben surprised her with a spontaneous kiss, she felt his passion excite every cell throughout her body.

When they reached the hill's crest, Ben had spread a picnic lunch for them and, exhilarated from the climb, they had savored the meal, the grandeur of the landscape, and their closeness.

Sterling's heart wobbled, remembering the raw emotion that had readily flowed between them like electricity.

Why am I doing this?

They'd watched a dramatic and roiling cloud formation overtake their sun-drenched day. Typical of Ben, he'd appreciated the exhilaration of a darkening sky as much as the blue sky. Gray clouds turned ominously dark with luminous orange backlighting an approaching tower of clouds. Sterling had urged him to follow her to the cabin they'd rented for the night, just a few yards down the trail.

She'd seen it in him then, that roaring rage that drove him, as he'd stood his ground while the winds worked up around him. Lightning flashed, striking a tree and dividing it in half, but Ben's excitement didn't waver. She'd even admired his audacity.

As rain began to pelt them, Ben finally grabbed her hand and led her to the cabin. She knew it wasn't that he didn't care about her well being as he stood in the powerful weather; it was that he completely gave himself to the experience and wanted the same for her. That evening, alone together in the cabin, Ben had asked her to marry him and she'd happily agreed.

Sterling turned away from the window, shaking her head to rid the thoughts that tormented her. Not long after that day, everything changed. Nicholas died two weeks later. With his death came the death of dreams for the life she'd planned.

A knock at the door scattered her thoughts. "Come in," she called.

"You always keep such late hours?" Ben strode into the office, still dressed in his deep blue suit. He fixed her with a piercing look.

As though challenged, she kept her eyes locked to his. "Actually, I was just getting ready to go home." There was no way he could have read the thoughts she'd been indulging in, but his look made her feel as if he somehow knew. Acutely.

"Going home? Can I give you a ride?" he offered, cocking his head to one side.

Sterling knew the beguiling move was unconscious on his part, but it pulled at her heart mercilessly. "No thanks. I have my car. What brought you up here?"

"I need to discuss the Pamela Witt murder with you."

"Again?"

"It can't be helped. It takes going over and over the details to ferret out the truth, remember?"

"You could have called, you know." Sterling chose to ignore his jab. He'd never made any bones that he didn't like her choice to leave the department.

"I like to do interviews face-to-face, don't you?" Ben's eyes glistened hypnotically.

Sterling knew all too well that Ben's motives were mixed, and she was not about to sit here helpless under his spell. Still, she had no choice but to cooperate, at least to some degree. He had her there. Resigned, she gathered her things, walked to the door and flipped off the light switch. City lights threw soft beams into the room, barely illuminating Ben's dark good looks. Pausing, she waited for him to follow. "We can talk on the way down."

"Have it your way. So how's Lacey's son?"

"He's doing okay. The doctor wanted to keep him in the hospital overnight, though, just to be sure."

"That's good to hear. Crazy kid," Ben said, shaking his head.

"He takes after his dad." Sterling looked away so Ben wouldn't see the emotions reverberating through her. Ben had worked on the force with Lacey's husband. He knew the man was fearless. Just like her father. Just like Ben.

"I'm sorry, Sterling," he said. "Tyler is such a good little guy and Lacey's already had it pretty rough."

She hated when he said the right thing. His voice sounded so deep and warm, nearly mesmerizing, like the melody of a favorite song.

Walking beside him, Sterling's nerves fairly screamed recognition of his masculine presence. She swallowed hard. "Did you get the coroner's report yet?" she asked, stepping into the elevator.

"Yeah. No surprises there. Of course, the coroner found water in her lungs, but Pamela died of strangulation."

Her eyes glued to the little number lights, Sterling watched them count backwards until the elevator reached the first floor. Six-five-four-three-two-one. She could feel Ben's eyes on her, and her heart beat a loud cadence in her ears.

"So the perp strangled her--"

"With his hands," Ben interrupted. "Like this."

He stepped in front of her and put his brawny hands around her neck. His eyes drew hers upward. The warmth was there, just like she remembered it. *God help me!*

Sterling lifted Ben's hands from her neck, and felt herself tremble. She hated it. His skin felt so inviting against her fingers. "We're on the ground floor, Ben."

Ben dropped his hands to his sides and stepped off the elevator. Thoughtfully, he rubbed his thumb against his chin. The rasping of his thick beard stubble sounded crisply inside Sterling's head, drawing her in like a bee to honey.

"We found Jerry's fingerprints on a glass in the bathroom," he said, eyeing her as she stepped out into the night.

Sterling cleared her throat. "So they were enjoying a little early morning tryst. That would explain why there was no sign of forced entry and why the dog didn't attack the killer. The dog must have known the killer. It seems pretty open and shut, huh?"

"Maybe," hedged Ben.

"Maybe a little too neat?"

"Yeah. But then, what's wrong with neat?"

"Well, here's my car," she said, stepping several feet away from Ben. Sterling pointed her remote key towards her car and put her hand on the door handle. Her hands still trembling despite her efforts to calm herself. Nervously, she glanced over her shoulder and saw Ben standing on the other side of the lot.

"You know, it seems like you're always walking away from me," he said, his voice low.

Instantly, Sterling pivoted. "Don't do that." She faced him with as much composure as she could muster.

"Don't do what?" A few succinct broad strides and he closed the distance between them.

"Don't keep referring to the past."

"I can't help it, Sterling. Maybe that's because what we shared isn't really in the past."

Standing close, he looked down at her with such sorrow, she wished she could reach out and hold him, tell him everything would be the way he wanted it. With strong emotions seething just under her skin, it would be so easy to tell him things could be the way they used to be.

Instead, she backed away. "Where's your car?"

"It's not here." With a shirk of his shoulders, Ben shoved his fists into his pockets. "I had a road officer drop me off."

"How were you going to give me a ride?" she asked, flabbergasted.

"Okay, so maybe I didn't think it through."

A smile got out and she started to chuckle. "You nut. Come on, I'll give you a ride to your apartment."

As Sterling pulled out of the parking space, Ben flashed her a wide smile. "Could we have dinner first? I'm famished."

"No. Just tell me where you live and I'll take you home."

"I live at the same place on State Street," he mumbled, settling into the seat.

Thank God he doesn't live far. I can't take much more of this. It took all of her determination to withstand the overpowering awareness of him charging the air.

Ben made attempts at small talk, for which Sterling felt grateful. Every time she opened her mouth she heard herself stammer like a child.

Silently, she pulled into a parking space outside of his apartment building. It felt like an eternity since she'd been here with him. But parts of her reacted like she was coming home.

"Maybe there is hope after all," Ben teased, his eyes glinting. "You still know the way. Maybe someday you'll be back -- to stay."

He climbed out of the car, and Sterling charged after him. She knew she shouldn't let him get to her, but this persistence had to stop.

Marching behind Ben up the stairs, Sterling fumed. "Why are you doing this, Ben Kirby?"

He said nothing.

"Don't ignore me." He unlocked the door and she stormed inside right behind him.

"Gee, come on in." Sarcasm dripped from his voice. "But watch out for the dog."

"Dog?" Sterling started, just as the streak of black and brown fur rambunctiously rounded the corner. "Mr. Teeth! What is he doing here? He's still limping?"

Ben crouched to corral the dog, and began scratching him affectionately under the chin. "The neighbors at the condo said his name is Joe, not Mr. Teeth. Somebody had to take him in. The animal control guys wanted to keep him, but he's our only witness to the Witt murder."

"Excuse me, did you say witness?"

"Yes, witness. And yes he's limping. The vet said he has a bruised muscle. Probably got kicked."

Sterling watched uneasily, thinking of stepping out through the still open front door. "Well that might explain why Lacey and I could get away from him at the condo, he had a lame leg. You two seem to have hit it off."

"He's not so ferocious once you get to know him. He's all bark. Besides, we have a lot in common. We're both trying to get over broken hearts."

Sterling's temper instantly flared. "It won't work, you know. Your little comments won't change anything. You're only driving me crazy!"

"I'm driving you crazy? I'm driving you crazy?" Ben stood to face her as Joe ambled away into the living room.

"Yes." Slamming her hands on her hips, Sterling stared Ben down. "Your comments keep bringing up old stuff. Stuff we settled two years ago."

In one second, he slammed the door shut and strode close to her. Standing inches from Sterling's face, Ben peered down at her. "We never settled anything. You may have, I don't know, but we never settled anything."

Ben's eyes locked hers and suddenly Sterling felt her walls tumble. The pain filling his face gripped her heart. She knew she caused it. She had never meant to hurt him so terribly. Doing the right thing shouldn't be so painful. Caught between the fear of what could happen and the agony of the moment, Sterling closed her eyes and collapsed against his chest. "I'm so sorry, Ben." Ben's body, rigid and hard, instantly drew up the buried cravings for his touch from deep and low inside her. As she let her mind relax, she felt a matching response, the taut muscles of his chest molding to her body.

"God, I've missed you," he breathed. Gently, reverently, he stroked her cheek, sending chills spiraling down her body.

"This can't be happening," she murmured, her eyes still closed. The intimate brush of his breath on her face sent reason swirling up in smoke.

"I love you, Sterling." His voice sounded raspy in her ear, emotion tumbling out. "I've never stopped."

With every kiss Ben pressed to her hair, Sterling's heart rose higher in her throat. His lips softly, hesitantly touched hers. They felt warm and so invitingly tender. Weakly, she pressed her face into the hollow of his neck as he nuzzled her hair. She breathed in the warm, earthy scent of Ben -- the only man who had ever gotten to her like this.

His touch opened a door she'd closed and fiercely guarded since the day she told him good-bye. All the emotions she'd let dam up poured out in a torrent that swept her along at a ferocious velocity. Her breath labored. She had to slow things down, think. Instead, she reached up to hold Ben's face between her hands, and found herself captured by the intense longing in his eyes.

Gripping her tightly, Ben seared her lips with a hard, hungry kiss. "There's been no one else, you know," he said, his voice thick.

Effortlessly, he wrapped Sterling in his arms, lifted her off her feet and carried her through the apartment to his bedroom. Gently, almost reverently, he laid her on his bed.Sterling felt his strength and knew he could overpower her. Ben stood above her, lean, agile, and assured, like a wildcat. But gentleness softened his power and she knew she wasn't his prey. Compelled by some deep hunger of her soul, she wanted this as much as he did.

His eyes -- dark blue pools of heat -- drew her in. Fears of the future drowned in those steady, simmering eyes. Ben pulled off his tie and shrugged off his suit coat. It fell silently to the floor and lay in a pool of moonlight filtering in through the window.

Starkly, his holster contrasted against his white shirt, reminding her: Danger rode on Ben's coat tails.

Quickly, he tossed the holstered gun into the corner, unbuttoned his shirt, and stripped naked. Just as quickly, the fearful thoughts were driven from her mind by the restless winds of passion Ben stirred inside her.

He lay down beside her and slid a warm hand inside her blouse, slipping it off one shoulder, then the other. Her breathing grew ragged as he took a nip of her shoulder. Traveling up to her waiting mouth, he teased it, taking his time to appreciate every sensuous delight.

Sterling couldn't stand it. The love she'd denied coursed through her body, firing her senses as though no time had passed. She wanted to feel him, all of him, with no holding back. She nipped at his ear, traced kisses down the angular line of his jaw, then gave life to her passion with a long, furious kiss.

Ben wrenched off her remaining clothes and pulled her on top of him. Sterling moaned instinctively as he ran a finger down her spine and caressed the small of her back. Hungrily, he kissed her lips, plunging his tongue to taste of her deeply. Delicious tremors shivered through her as their thighs slid side by side.

Slowly, Sterling raked her breasts against the curling dark mat on his chest, savoring the feel of Ben.

He took her breasts in his hands, cupping them firmly but gently, and stared transfixed. "So beautiful," he murmured and rubbed his thumb over a rosy circle. His mouth fastened to her, his tongue driving her passion. A low, primal moan escaped Ben's throat as he plunged his head between the soft swells, then grabbed hard of her head to face his smoldering gaze.

Ben's eyes held Sterling's, coaxing her to match his unabashed intensity. She felt carried along on a wild current of wind so strong, neither one could stop it. Nor wanted to.

Ben pulled her tight and gracefully rolled over on top of her. Her body arched with abandon and she plowed her fingers through his thick, dampened hair, pulling his head close. His lips pressed hot kisses to her abdomen, licked playfully at her navel, then trailed more kisses along her thigh, taking her faster and deeper into the center of her being where the perfect love waited. Unleashed, it felt so right. She wanted nothing but to fuse completely with him.

Urgent with need, Ben paused only long enough to ensure protection, but coming to her more fiercely, he melted to Sterling, meeting the aching inside her.

As one with Ben, Sterling felt the primal rhythm take her over. Her body rising and falling in synchrony with his, she reveled in the hardness of his sculpted muscles. Her breath was his breath. His tender musings were her thoughts.

As through riding with Ben on a wild wind, Sterling sailed higher and higher into a delicious paradise, where calmness and peace shuddered through her. Breathless and locked with Ben in intimate embrace, she tumbled with him straight downward toward earth, carried by the gentle breeze of satisfaction. Exhausted, she felt a contented rest take her over.

CHAPTER 6

"*Y*ou should try to get some sleep. We'll keep an eye on your son and if there's any problem we'll wake you. But he's doing just fine," said Tyler's nurse, who was making her nightly rounds. "I'd be happy to make up the hide-a-bed for you."

Even in the dim light from the hall Lacey could see the woman's eyes were kind. "Thanks. This chair will be fine."

"At least take this blanket."

As the nurse closed the door behind her, Lacey huddled down deeper into the upholstered chair and unfolded the blanket across her lap. Lacey knew the nurse had no way of knowing that it didn't matter where she rested her head, she would not be sleeping tonight.

The soft sounds of Tyler's breathing comforted her. The steady rhythm, in and out, in and out, assured Lacey that her son's accident was just a bump in the road, not another tragedy. But even though sleeplessness ached at the back of her eyes, she would remain vigilant, like a sentry at the watch. It was the only way to make sure nothing would rob her of her cherished loved one.

Thirty minutes later with her strained muscles begging for a stretch, Lacey unfurled from the chair and walked to the window, the blanket pulled around her shoulders. A starless, dark sky blanketed the night, but Lacey suspected the stars, hidden in the glow of the city lights, were twinkling brightly. Invisible, but always there.

Lacey felt a tickle against her ear as one of the rose quartz earring her sister had given her twisted gently. A shiver shimmied down her spine and her attention was drawn to an image reflected in the window. She blinked hard, twice. The blanket slipped from her fingers and cascaded around her feet. "Nicholas?" Freezing to the spot facing the window, Lacey squeezed her eyes shut. "You're really letting your imagination run wild, Lacey," she said, talking to herself out loud and not daring to open her eyes.

Then she smelled it. The subtle sweetness of apple blossoms made familiar by association.

The scent reminded her of a loved voice, a strong shoulder, a sweet smile. And, oh, how much she'd missed it all. She stood captured in the implausibility of the moment.

"No, you're not imagining anything, honey."

Still facing the window, Lacey slowly opened her eyes, a delicious feeling of finding something once lost lighting in her heart. "Nicholas," she breathed. Her husband's unmistakable sparkling eyes reflecting back at her melted all disbelief. "But how...Is this magic?"

Lacey felt his touch on her shoulder, so warm and known, and chanced to turn and look directly at her beloved Nicholas, or at least at the dream of him.

"No, it's not magic, it's love. Don't worry about how. Just know I'm here now, Lacey." Nick drew her into his arms. "I've missed you so much."

There was no mistaking it, this was really Nicholas. Once a woman is connected to a man the way she had been connected to her Nick, his presence is known as surely as she would know her own home.

Nestled against his chest, all the fears and longings Lacey had been carrying around for two years seeped away into thin air.

"Oh, how I've longed for this," she said.

"I know. I felt it too," Nick said, gently stroking her hair. "I had to find a way to reach you."

Lacey made herself pull away from his embrace. "I have so many questions. But I'm afraid."

Nick cupped her face in his hand and tilted her chin up to him. Closing his eyes, he pressed a tender kiss to her lips, sending her senses spiraling. It had been so long since she'd felt so loved. Tears welled from her eyes and drifted down her cheeks.

"Don't be afraid, Lacey," Nick said, brushing away her tears. "And don't cry, love. I'm never far away, now. And I promise I'll answer all your questions."

Fear instantly ignited in her heart. "You're leaving aren't you."

"I have to go, but don't worry, I'll be back. Nothing can keep me from you, Lacey. Just believe that."

In an instant, it was as if Nicholas was only a mirage. Lacey stood in the hospital room, alone with the sounds of her sleeping son.

Sterling rolled over in bed, the rich aroma of coffee filling her head. She stretched lazily, opened her eyes and gazed around Ben's bedroom.

"Good morning, beautiful," Ben greeted, sauntering into the room with the German shepherd padding closely behind him.

The scent of Ben freshly showered wafted around her as he bent low and laid a kiss to her cheek. It was a scent that had always been heady medicine to her. "You shouldn't have let me sleep so late," Sterling said, glancing at the clock beside the bed.

"Seven-thirty. Yeah, that's real late, you lazy thing," he teased, standing in front of the dresser and adjusting his collar to fit his tie.

"I notice you're dressed." A hint of guilt plucked at her conscious. *I should be dressed and ready for work, too, instead of lying here naked in Ben's bed.* Was it her imagination, or did he seem a little distant?

"You know me. I get restless if I stay in bed too long. Are you ready for coffee or would you like to shower first?"

"The coffee smells great. I'll come out in the kitchen." Sterling caught his look in her radar. What is he thinking, she wondered.

"Okay, you know where my robe is, so help yourself. And take your time." He walked out the door and headed to the kitchen without a backward glance.

Ben's blue terrycloth robe snugged around her body, Sterling padded barefoot through the apartment and sat in the kitchen chair where he'd set a mug of coffee on the table. She nestled both hands around the cup and drew a mouthful. The hot liquid tasted wonderful. He sure knew how to make a good cup of coffee. She slowly sipped it, all the while peering at Ben as he set breakfast in front of her.

"Western omelet and a slice of wheat toast," he said, sitting down to his own plate across the table from her.

"You remembered how I like it," she mused.

"Oh, you need a fork."

Automatically, Sterling reached for the utensil drawer and pulled out forks for both of them.

"You remembered." Ben's eyes bored inside her.

Sterling shifted uncomfortably in her chair and glanced around the small kitchen. From the old silver toaster to the plain white cotton curtains at the window, the kitchen looked as she remembered it. "You haven't changed things."

"That's true." He took a gulp of coffee to wash down his eggs. "I haven't really thought much about wallpaper patterns or curtains."

The phone on the wall rang and Ben jumped up to get it. No question, the department was on the other end. Sterling tuned out the words he spoke as all of her attention converged on the sight of him. The tilt of his head, the glossy darkness of his hair, the way he held his mouth in concentration.

Ben turned to look at her, unleashed a smile, and winked.

Sterling's pulse jumped a dizzying degree. Ben seemed so profoundly alive. She'd missed that. It would be so easy to step back into his life. To hardly miss a beat. Like putting the remote on pause, then turning the movie back on without affecting the story at all.

Ben hung up the phone and walked around the table, pulling Sterling to her feet. Placing his hands on her hips, he drew her to him and brushed her lips with his. The kiss felt sweet and coaxing. A nuzzle in her hair brought the sound of his breathing up close, wrapping around her thoughts and tugging at her heart. She remembered so many things. His zest for living. His boundless self-confidence. And how when they were together his careless disregard for safety had intrigued her and excited her as much as it had frightened her. *He says he's changed.*

Sterling closed her eyes and saw his apartment. Newspapers piled in small heaps around the living room. Dishes stacked on the kitchen counter. Damp towels lying carelessly on the bathroom floor. All indications that the slightly tamed Ben Kirby retained much of his former self.

Uninvited sensations shimmered through her, set in motion by Ben's insistent kisses to her neck. He looked down at her, one finger softly tracing the upward tilt of her nose.

Trembling, Sterling pulled back. "This is all too easy. I walked right back in as though nothing has changed."

Ben released her, staring at her through hollow eyes, his jaw tight.

Turning away, she took in a deep breath and let it out slowly. "I know where you keep your things. I know this place as well as I know my own apartment. It would be so easy to go on from here." Whirling to face him, Sterling tried to calm the fears threatening to choke her. "But nothing has changed. The reason I couldn't be with you is still there. There is no happy ending for people like us." Now she knew what had been in his eyes earlier. He'd already suspected she would come to her senses.

"What, you're going to pretend last night never happened?"

"That's right," she stormed. "It shouldn't have happened."

"But it did. And it meant something, Sterling. At least it did to me."

It scared her how much emotion raged inside her. She didn't want to think about how close to the edge she felt, how vulnerable.

Ben shook his head. "You can't spend your whole life shoring up against getting hurt."

Speechless, Sterling tried harder to wall off her mind, her heart. Ben was too close. "Do you think you've figured out something? It's an interesting theory, Ben, but it doesn't hold water."

"You don't know the future, Sterling. Nothing is going to happen to me, Sterling." His voice sounded quiet, collected.

"Right!" she spouted. "You must have forgotten, I've heard that before, many times. I saw what my mother went through year after year, worrying if my father would come home for dinner. He told her not to worry. It didn't mean anything." Hot tears stung her eyes, but angry, she willed them to stop.

"Sterling, tell me you don't love me."

Silence churned between them. How could she tell him that? But could she survive loving him? "You're trying to change the subject. Love can come and it can go. And it can drive you nuts on a lonely night. Just ask Lacey."

"Tell me you love me," he demanded, slamming his fist against the table, his calmness evaporating. "If you loved me, we could deal with the job."

"I know I thought I could deal with it. Heck, when we met, I was a cop too, just like my dad."

"Sterling--"

"It really happens, Ben. Cops get killed. My mother's worst nightmare became reality. Dad got shot." She heard her voice wobble, but she couldn't stop the angry words. "Then, when a bullet took Nicholas' life, I saw it all again -- the pain and loss Lacey suffered, just like Mom. Lacey's alone, just like Mom. You know that's why I had to quit the police force. That's why I had to break up with you. I had to put all that behind me. I don't want to end up a cop's widow. I don't want to be the wreckage left behind."

Ben shook his head and shuffled his weight from one foot to the other. "Sterling, I've changed. I don't work undercover anymore. You know that. Things are different."

"You can put on a suit and tie, Ben, but that doesn't change the man you are. How long will you be content working investigations?"

"It's been six months." His brow furrowed.

"I used to warn you to drop your flamboyant ways or you'd end up in the morgue. You and that equally crazy partner of yours, what was his name? Jay Thomas. You always challenged the odds. That's who you are. Like a fearless warrior -- fearless and foolish. It scares me." Sterling narrowed her eyes and stared at Ben, not quite understanding the sullen look coloring his face.

He turned his back to her, his strong shoulders drooping. "You don't know, do you?"

"What are you talking about?"

"Jay is crippled."

"What?" A rock the size of a baseball dropped into the pit of her stomach.

"You were right." Ben turned tormented eyes to her. "We challenged the odds and someday we'd pay, you used to say. Well, my partner did pay."

"I didn't know," Sterling said, taking Ben's hand in hers and holding it to her cheek. The weather in the room had suddenly shifted. She couldn't help but move to console him. "When?"

"Six months ago," he said, flatly. "We were following a lead for a big drug bust and happened on a domestic dispute. The guy was strung out and the thing went bad. Jay got shot. The bullet shattered his knee. His life is never going to be the same. He works a desk job at the department now."

"I'm so sorry Ben," she said, instantly certain of his self-recrimination. Another thing that never changed. "I'm sure it wasn't your fault."

"You know nothing of the kind." He spit out the words as though ridding his mouth of a foul taste.

The pain inside him pulsed so strong, Sterling sensed it took all Ben's energy just to keep breathing in and out. Jay and Ben had been like brothers. "Why didn't you call me? I would have been there for you."

"Why would I? You made it clear you didn't want to be part of my life." His eyes hardened. "So that's when I moved to investigations. I knew I didn't have nine lives and I'd already used up several. I didn't want to ruin anyone else's life, although it seems to be my thing in life, doesn't it?"

She knew he wasn't talking just about Jay. Sorrow and death had accompanied Ben from youth, just like it had her.

Running the back of his hand across her lips, Sterling closed her eyes and imagined she could will his pain away. "I've hurt you so much." She hadn't realized until just now that she'd inflicted such a deep, ragged wound.

"You don't need to blame yourself. You had no idea. Besides, it's my problem."

Wrapping her arms around his neck, she leaned against him, listening to the steady beat of his heart. Could she ever make up for hurting him so? Last night had been intoxicating – a dream. Today reality set in, warning her to get out quick. To put Ben and all the fearsome possibilities he brought with him in her review mirror. Now, faced with Ben's bleeding heart, what could she, should she do? "Ben, I--"

He put a finger to her lips. "Don't say it. I want to be with you more than anything I've ever wanted. But I want you to be happy too, Sterling. Pity won't cut it. If you can't tell me you love me, well, it won't work, will it?"

Sterling's heart squeezed painfully, torn between the soft spot in her soul for Ben and the stubborn demand for self-survival driving her. Lowering her gaze to the floor, she stepped out of his arms.

A resigned scowl darkened his face. "So, that's the way it is." Ben turned to the counter and grabbed a dishtowel. His mental and emotional shift was visible as he squared his shoulders. "Well, I better get this mess cleaned up or I'll be late for work."

Silently, Sterling treaded back to the bedroom and searched for her clothes.

God help me to do the thing I need to do, she prayed. I keep hurting him, but I can't believe being with him is right. It wouldn't be anything more than a quick fix that would end up badly.

Buttoning up the last button of her blouse, Sterling stared into the bureau mirror. *Put your head on straight. You have a case to solve.*

The case. The work. That's where things would fall into place and she could easily navigate her life without fear of the inevitable and insufferable pain. Working the case was in her blood just as surely as plasma and corpuscles. It was second nature. Something she could fall into wholeheartedly and not have to think.

Or feel.

Quietly, Sterling patted Joe's head and ruffled his ears before she let herself out of Ben's apartment.

"How are we coming with that Witt murder?"

His sergeant's question pierced Ben's thoughts as he sat behind his desk at the police station. "I'm moving slowly. You know, the guy we like for doing it is pretty well known in certain circles of Laurelwood."

"What's his name? Jerry Rutheford? Yeah, of course he's pretty known." The serg.'s gravelly voice spoke of too many years of too many cigarettes. "He's a top dog at the Laurelwood County State Bank."

"He and his wife seem to have kept pretty much to themselves, but he's done his share of public relations, so the community knows him."

"Why are we focusing on him?" The sergeant patted his pockets but came up empty. "You smoke? I could sure use a cigarette. Course, I'm trying to quit."

Ben chuckled. How many times had he heard that? "We identified his fingerprints at the scene. According to a private investigator hired by the guy's wife, he and the victim had been having an affair."

"What's the motive?"

"I'm still working on it." Ben downed a swallow of his lukewarm coffee and frowned. He would be the first to admit that his concentration wasn't on full. Well, at least not when it came to the investigation. Sterling was an entirely different matter.

"Keep at it." Distracted, the sergeant moved to the next room to answer a call.

Sighing, Ben looked around the busy room. Officers moving in and out. Phones ringing. Everything seemed strictly business. No one could know that before Sgt. Rogard caught him, his thoughts verged on the edge of indecent. Sterling had taken him over.

Last night had been the fulfillment of two year's waking and sleeping dreams. Touching her, lying beside her had felt like taking in much needed water for his thirsty soul.

Being near Sterling had reminded him how hard he'd worked at shoving his feelings deep enough to ignore. When she stepped into his life again, he quickly knew he'd been fooling himself. All the feelings ignited with the lilt of her step and the flip of her luxurious locks.

Ben's gut ached, remembering the sweetness of waking early in the morning and simply watching Sterling sleep. Listening to her soft breathing had nearly driven him nuts and he'd wrestled with the longing to pull her into his arms again.

When he'd held her at breakfast, he'd taken in and savored every bit of her -- her silky skin, her sweet scent, her pure and vibrant essence. He'd wanted to believe things had changed and Sterling would stay in his life.

But they'd always thought alike. *Damn it.* He'd known her doubt. She'd looked up into his face wearing the same look she'd worn the day they parted. The powerful sadness glinting in Sterling's beautiful blue-green eyes still knotted his stomach. The love he felt for her nearly ate him up. But it wasn't enough. She had to love him the same way, holding no doubts.

"Kirby, do you hear me? There's someone to see you."

Startled, Ben brought his attention to the officer tapping his shoulder. It was Jay. "Sorry. Who is it?" he asked rising.

"Mrs. Sara Rutherford." Jay motioned to the woman standing across the room. "You okay, Ben?"

Jay's question sounded interested, something Ben hadn't heard from him in a while. "Sure. Just tired."

"Have some more coffee, buddy. You look terrible," Jay joked as let the door to the room close behind him.

Things were so different since the accident. In another time Ben might have shared the truth with Jay. That the chasm between his dearest wishes of last night and reality of today was splitting him open. But he knew better than to reach out to his former partner now.

"Hello, Mrs. Rutherford." Ben tossed off his turmoil and stepped in the woman's direction. "Let's go into the conference room. We can talk better there."

The woman's eyes were wide and tinged with fright. Ben led her into a private room and closed the door. "Have a seat," he said, motioning to a chair at the table. "I want to thank you for coming down to the station to talk. I know this is probably all a little overwhelming."

"That's okay. When I got your call, I came right down. I don't know what help I can be, though. I haven't seen or spoken with my husband for three days." Sara swallowed hard. "Jerry's secretary said he called and told her he had to go on an unexpected business trip. He didn't call me."

"Is that normal? I mean, for your husband not to contact you?"

"Not really."

"What about the business trip. Where did he go?" Ben had already spoken with Jerry's secretary, but had gotten no real answers.

"His secretary said she thought he had a meeting in Chicago. But she seemed nearly as in the dark as me."

Ben twirled his pen and eyed the woman. The picture of innocence and frailty. Yet his instincts told him something didn't fit. "Why the unexpected trip? Did that sort of thing happen much?"

"Never. Jerry always had at least a day's notice, usually more." Sara sat rigid in the chair, chewing her lower lip. "I'm sorry I can't tell you more."

Ben stood and walked to the other side of the room. The scent of old coffee and industrial cleaner hung in the station air like smog. But it was familiar, and somehow helped him focus on the case when all he wanted to do was go to Sterling. "What were you doing at nine a.m. the day of the murder?"

Nearly imperceptibly, Sara flinched. She drew in a deep breath. "I can't say exactly. I rose at seven o'clock, showered, and ate breakfast. Jerry had already left for work, or at least that's what I thought."

"Okay. Then what?" Ben shoved his hand into his pocket and pulled out some change, directing his eyes to the nickels, dimes, and quarters.

"I worked in my garden," she said simply.

He put the coins back into his pocket. He didn't know what he hoped to discover by talking to the woman. She seemed so flat, so devoid of hopes and dreams. But did that make her an accomplice to murder? "It's getting to be that time of year, isn't it? What time did you work in your garden?"

"Maybe about ten-thirty. I don't know for sure."

"You didn't talk with anyone or see anyone?"

"No. Not until Lacey and Sterling called me later in the day."

"And why was that? What did they want?"

Sara cleared her throat and stared at the floor. "They asked me to come to their office. After I got there, they confirmed that Jerry had been having an affair with Pamela and they told me they'd found her dead." Directing a clearly pained expression at him, she continued. "I believe this is all the same information I told another officer that same day."

"I understand. I'm sorry to ask you to go over the sequence of events again. I'm trying to figure out where your husband could be, Mrs. Rutherford. Can you help me with that?"

"If you're asking me would I tell you if I knew, the answer would be I don't know, Detective. I know that's not what you want to hear, but, after all, he is my husband. And I would like to talk to him myself."

This was the most spunk he'd seen in Sara since meeting her. "So you're saying your husband hasn't contacted you, right?"

Sara sighed and again bit her lower lip. "No, he has not."

"No phone calls, no visits." Maybe if he kept at her, she'd give up something useful.

"I guess there is one thing that seems odd," Sara said, looking up quizzically into his face. "Jerry didn't take any clothes with him to Chicago."

"You know that for sure?" There it was. The little bit of new information that makes persistence pay off.

Again, she sighed. "Yes. Our marriage may seem pretty lacking to you, but I do know when my husband has packed clothes for out of town. I guess I should have thought to mention it before."

"That's understandable. You've had some pretty unsettling news to deal with. Thanks again for cooperating, Mrs. Rutherford. I appreciate your patience." Ben opened the door and waited for Sara to lead out.

She paused halfway through the doorway. "Detective, are you certain my husband killed that woman?"

"We're still investigating," he answered, his hand on the doorknob.

"But you found his fingerprints in her home, right?" she pressed.

"That's right. But given the nature of their relationship, that would not be considered conclusive evidence."

Sara looked down. "I understand."

Ben walked her to the front desk and told her good-bye. "Don't leave town, Mrs. Rutherford. We may need to talk some more."

She looked over her shoulder, her eyes solid, unflinching. "Do you think I killed that woman, Detective?"

"We're investigating everyone connected to the parties, Mrs. Rutherford. It's standard procedure."

"I understand."

Turning back to the pile of papers stacked on his desk, Ben shrugged into his seat, Sara Rutherford's face still in his mind.

He wasn't sure if he didn't believe her innocence because it was too easy or because his compass was off. *That's what happens when you let your mind wander off work and start feeling sorry for yourself, man.*

Pains in his chest twisted and words echoed up from the past.

"I love you Ben. But when will you deal with the demons that drive you? What are you afraid of?"

"I'm not afraid of anything, Sterling."

"Don't give me that. You don't have to prove anything to me. But you have to face your fears before the demons will go away."

She'd been like that, always pushing him to explore what made him tick. She knew his past was a cocklebur in his side. But they had always ended up in the same spot. The spot where one boy died and another did not.

"If you could see yourself as I see you, things would be different, Ben."

In his mind's eye Ben could still see the love shining warmly from Sterling's beautiful eyes that night. Feeling so undeserving, he'd made a joke.

Ben shoved the pile of papers aside with a swift brush of his arm. He hadn't realized that the love would go away.

CHAPTER 7

"*H*i, Sterling, I'm calling to give you an update on your nephew."

Sterling relaxed at her desk. Lacey's voice lilted cheerily, so she happily thought things must be looking up."Okay, let's have it."

"Tyler is doing much better. In fact, he may come home from the hospital tomorrow."

"That's a great report. I suppose he'll be grounded for life?" Sterling teased.

"I've been considering it."

"Can you put him on the phone?"

"Sure, sis."

"Hi, Aunt Sterling." The little voice over the phone sent Sterling's heart soaring.

"Hi, champ. What's this I hear you tried out your wings and got a silly bump on your head?"

The delightful giggle assured Sterling that her nephew was on the mend.

"I don't have any wings, Aunt Sterling. I wish I did, because then I could fly out of here." The little guy's voice lost its happy and turned glum. "There's nothing to do here and Mom won't let me get out of bed even."

"Not even get out of bed? You poor sweetie," she gushed, imagining her little nephew's patience waning. He had to be pretty sick to be willing to sit still for any length of time, so his restlessness was a good sign. "Well you get all rested and when you come home, you and I will do something fun. You can be thinking about what you want to do."

"Could we go get pizza? The food here has been sort of yucky."

"Sure we could."

"Just you and me?" Excitement bubbled in Tyler's voice.

"Just you and me, cutie. Kisses!"

"Kisses! Here's Mom."

"Sounds like you and my son are making a date. Thanks for cheering him up, Sterling."

"My pleasure. He's my favorite little guy, you know."

"Yeah, I know."

Sterling detected weariness in her sister's voice. And something else. "How are you holding up, sis?"

"Don't worry about me, Sterling. I'm better than I have been in a long time. You could say it's kind of a miracle."

"You know I don't believe in miracles. But I do believe in you. You're pretty resilient, and apparently so is your little son." Sterling sensed something under the radar about her sister, but decided against pursuing it over the phone.

"So how are things coming with Sara's case? Or should I say Jerry's case?"

Sterling straightened her back. "I'm looking into various aspects of the investigation."

"Wow. That was pat. Why do I suspect you're holding something back, sis?"

"Because you have a suspicious nature?" Sterling could easily imagine her sister's face lighting with curiosity. It wasn't that she was meddlesome, just took the role of "Big Sister" seriously and always had.

"I know an evasion when I hear one. Okay, I won't pry. But you have to promise to fill me in on what's going on, because I know something is."

"Lacey, you know I wouldn't hold back information on a case."

"I'm not referring to the case."

"Oh."

Lacey laughed. "You can't escape me. I'm only interested in your best interest, especially where Ben Kirby is concerned."

"Hadn't you better check on my nephew or something?" Sterling asked, almost wishing her sister could guide her when it came to Ben. She dearly loved her sister and respected her. Unfortunately, when it came to matters of the heart, Lacey was all emotion, no logic. Sensible was what Sterling needed, not fairy dust and rainbows. "Besides, I'm trying to focus on the case."

"I know," Lacey said, sounding sympathetic. "I'll be in to work as soon as I can."

Sterling hung up the phone and adjusted her thoughts. *Unless I want to let Lacey down, I'd better figure out what's happened to my client's husband.*

But it would take more than determination to make room in Sterling's thoughts for Sara's problems with her husband. Ben called to her. Relentlessly. She knew him too well to be able to completely deaden herself to his needs.

Sterling ran her fingers through her hair, restless with the gnawing truths of Ben's life. Not many people knew that the passion driving his police work sprang from self-inflicted pain. Ben kept his past to himself.

But Sterling knew all about it. She knew that he'd lived with death as she had. That his parents had been killed in a car accident when he was nine. That he'd been sent to live with an aunt and uncle. And only she knew that the uncle abused Ben and blamed him for the accidental death of his cousin.

Sterling reviewed the facts in her head just as a police officer would, but with none of the detachment. Ben's story still touched her heart.

The two boys had snuck away from chores and had been swimming in a nearby creek on a hot summer afternoon. But the fun turned tragic when Ben's cousin jumped off a bridge into the creek and hit his head on a rock. Ben had jumped in and pulled the boy out of the water, but death had come instantaneously with a broken neck.

Ben had suffered the blame simply because he'd broken the rules to enjoy a little fun, a little freedom. His uncle had dealt harshly with him. What was worse, Ben accepted the blame. It drove him, a mindless compulsion, always trying to right the wrong he felt responsible for.

Sterling's heart cringed, knowing the pain Ben carried and remembering the night he'd shared it with her.

"You don't understand, Sterling. It was my fault my cousin died. My uncle was right. I'm bad news."

"You were just a kid, Ben, doing normal kid things. You deserve so much more out of life than carrying around mistaken guilt."

"You don't understand. How can I ever make it right? It was all my fault."

She wondered, would Ben continue to blame himself for the rest of his life?

Sterling shook her head to banish the thoughts of Ben. She couldn't erase the past. She had her own problems and she knew she couldn't live never feeling safe from the moment of learning of his death.

Maybe I do love Ben. But love won't shield me or him from the bullet that takes his life. That was her truth.

Nothing had changed. Her work needed her attention and her work was where she could control her life.

Jerry Rutherford's daily planner sat in front of her; the odd-looking key confiscated from his desk lay beside it. It struck her as slightly peculiar that the man relied on such a low-tech tool as the planner. But she couldn't question it too much. Unlike many of their contemporaries, she and Lacey had little patience with computers, much less the many gadgets available to their profession. Give her something solid she could put her fingers on and feel her senses with, like a leather-bound planner, any day.

She'd been pondering the two objects for hours, but their secrets wouldn't budge.

Jerry's life seemed on the surface to be pretty predictable. Work, meetings, lunches, more work, and more meetings. Sterling had first hoped the planner would reveal names and addresses or the whereabouts of a safety deposit box to fit the key. Of course, in her fantasy, this safety deposit box would somehow lead her directly to Jerry.

No such luck.

Drumming a pencil on the top of her desk, Sterling's mind drew down to a focused spot inside herself. How did the pieces of this case fit together, she wondered. Why would Jerry have killed his mistress? To where had he disappeared? Short of the earth swallowing him up, the man had to be somewhere. She just had to think.

Then she knew. To solve this case, she must go back to the beginning. To Pamela Witt's condo.

STERLING PARKED her car a few blocks away from the condo and slipped into the backyard. Sure the cops wouldn't be too pleased to know what she had in mind but she had to look around.

Getting inside was no problem. She jimmied the lock on the patio door and slid in. This time only the stale air of the closed-up condo met her, rather than the huge dog, Mr. Teeth, a.k.a, Joe.

The place had already been searched by the LPD, Sterling knew. They'd collected evidence and scoured the condo for information. Nothing had come of it yet. Of course, the cops already thought they had their killer; they just needed to identify a motive. Her gut told her to look for herself. To look beyond the obvious.

Sterling headed straight down the white-carpeted hallway to the pale pink bedroom. The brass bed lay unmade, its rose- colored comforter tossed carelessly at the foot, no doubt closely the way it was left the morning Pamela died.

Sterling pulled open the door to the expansive walk-in closet, flipped on the light switch, and walked inside. Designer shoes of every color sat neatly in little stacked cubicles on one end. She thumbed through the many clothes hanging along the walls and noted their expensive labels.

Outside the closet stood a mahogany dresser. Riffling through the dresser drawers, Sterling didn't know exactly what she hoped to find, but she did uncover more information about Pamela. *Cashmere sweaters and designer underwear. This woman sure had expensive taste.*

Sterling pursed her lips and scanned the room and its contents in a long, deliberate sweep. *Hmm. Something's missing. There's no jewelry box.*

Now Sterling knew what she came for. A woman like Pamela would unquestionably own jewelry. And it would be lovely, extravagantly priced jewelry. Beautiful gold chains, pearls, and gemstones, she imagined. The kind of stuff kept in a safe, Sterling thought, and didn't even bother to look behind any of the pictures hanging on the walls.

She went to the closet and shoved aside the clothes. Nothing. No, she thought, that would be too obvious. Deftly, she felt along the edges of the wooden shoe cubicles.

Bingo. Her efforts were rewarded with finding a lever discreetly hidden in the beveled edge of one of the cubbyholes. Sterling pulled out the red leather pumps sitting there and pressed the lever. A door at the back of the cubbyhole popped open, revealing the contents of the safe. Boxes. She opened one, then another and found what she'd expected. Costly jewelry.

A large envelope lying along the wall of the safe caught Sterling's attention and she reached for it.

Suddenly Sterling felt a cold chill sweep over her body. She stopped and listened. Was someone in the condo? Slowly, she peeked out of the closet, the uneasy feeling still sitting at the pit of her stomach.

But only the sound of birds chirping outside the bedroom windows met her ears.

Still spooked, Sterling stepped back into the closet, quickly pulled out the envelope from the safe and took a look at the contents. Satisfied, she stuffed the envelope under her jacket, closed the safe, and returned the shoes to the cubbyhole.

Swiftly, she closed the closet door and stole down the hallway, past the bathroom, and through the kitchen. A breath of fresh air brushed her face and she froze, her gaze frantically searching for its origin.

Adrenaline coursed through her, heightening her senses.

There it was. Lace curtains delicately floated on a sweet spring breeze wafting in through an open window in the den. A window that had not been open moments ago when she entered the condo. Did this mean the rooster had come home, she wondered.

Stealthily, Sterling retraced her steps to the bedroom, looking behind each door and every drape for the intruder, expecting to find the wayward husband Jerry.

When she felt satisfied no one remained hiding somewhere in the condo she scrutinized the windowsill for fingerprints. *Damn it. Completely clean.*

Certain she wasn't mistaken about an intruder, Sterling stepped into the afternoon sunshine and glanced around the lawn and nearby houses.

Sunlight filtered through the leaves of maple and oak trees. A slight wind tossed the daffodils and tulips blooming in the yard next door. Nothing seemed out of the ordinary, but still the creepy feeling weighed heavy inside her.

As she closed the back porch door, she had all she could do to keep from bolting to her car parked down the street.

"WHOA!" Ben nearly collided with Sterling at the back corner of the condo. Instinctively, he put his hands to her shoulders to keep from hurting her.

She turned wide, frightened eyes up at him. "Ben! What are you doing here?"

He dropped his hands. In a moment, he'd pull her close but she didn't want that. Not even if she felt scared down to her beautiful toes. "What am I doing here? Wait a minute, babe. What are you doing here?"

Sterling seemed uneasy, shifting her gaze away from him. "Don't get all hot and bothered," she spouted. "I'm investigating, remember?" She glanced over her shoulder at the back porch.

"What brought you here?" Ben couldn't help but follow the direction of her eyes. The porch seemed unremarkable, with only the lilac bushes swaying in the wind catching his attention.

"I don't know," she hedged. "Just--"

"A hunch," he interjected. "I know. I feel the same way, but I can't put my finger on it. I thought I'd give the place another once over." Sterling still refused to give him eye contact. Ben's stomach knotted. *She probably would like to avoid me, the sorry, lovesick guy who keeps bugging her.*

"Well, I'll see you later, Ben. I've got to go." Sterling skirted around him and headed stiffly away.

"Where's your car?"

"Down the street," she called without slowing her steps.

He watched her slightly swaying hips, her gray skirt slimly silhouetting her curves. Sunshine glinted off her soft spun hair. "Wait, Sterling."

She didn't stop.

Ben took off after her in an easy jog, not knowing why exactly, other than being close to Sterling made his heart sing. Taking hold of her arm, he turned her to face him. A manila envelope dropped from under her jacket.

Sterling glanced up at him, then quickly stooped to pick it up.

"What's that?" Suddenly her uneasiness made sense.

"Nothing."

"I think it's something. Are you withholding evidence? Where did you get that? Did you go inside. Need I remind you that's an unlawful entry?" Ben knew he shouldn't be surprised. Sterling would do what she felt she had to for her client.

But the cop in him didn't like it.

"I don't have to tell you anything, Ben." Her eyes flashed defiantly.

"Have you forgotten everything you learned on the force? You're required to turn over anything that is related the case. In case you've forgotten, obstructing justice is a crime."

"Don't talk to me like that, like I'm some stupid rookie." Sterling turned on her heels and marched away.

Ben stepped up alongside her. "Sterling, you're compromising the investigation. Hand over the envelope and whatever else you're hiding."

"No. I'm investigating. That's what I do. I haven't even looked at what's inside yet. Not really. And I'm not hiding anything." Pulling a key from her skirt pocket, Sterling unlocked her car.

As she opened the door, Ben stepped between Sterling and the vehicle. "Then let's have a look right now."

"Not here," she said, again, uneasily glancing around.

Again, Ben followed her look. "Look out!" he hollered, hauling her to the side of the car and slamming his body against hers. A black sedan barreled down on them, then swerved, nearly ripping off Sterling's driver side door.

"What the hell?" Sterling sputtered into his ear, seemingly completely unmindful of the frenzy he felt at her closeness. "Let me up!"

"Sorry. I was only trying to protect you." Standing, Ben ran to the middle of the street to catch a glimpse of the sedan.

"I can take care of myself," she retorted, climbing behind the wheel and starting the engine.

"Hey, where are you going?"

Pulling into the street, Sterling rolled her window down and shot him a look. "Where do you think? I'm going after the guy who just tried to run us down." Sterling squealed the tires in a fast break.

"Wait. I'm coming with you." Breaking into a sprint, Ben grabbed the passenger door handle and pulled.

"What are you doing," Sterling hollered as he jumped into the passenger seat and slammed the door closed.

"I told you, I'm going with you. Can't you go any faster?" Ben pounded his fists on the dash. "He's getting away. Can you make out the plate?"

Sterling glanced briefly over at him, and their eyes held for a moment. Excitement sparked brightly in the beautiful blue-green pools, pushing his adrenaline higher. This was the way it used to be. Together they'd reveled in life's thrills. Giving chase to an idiot driver definitely qualified as a thrill.

Then the look vanished, and she directed her attention to the road again.

Snaking around slower-moving cars, Sterling closed the gap between them and the sedan. Horns from other cars blared at them as they swerved from lane to lane.

"Step on it, Sterling. I want to see this guy face to face."

"I'm doing the best I can, officer. You should have taken your car and used a code three, with all the lights and sirens. And you could have called for back-up."

"Screw back-up. We'll get this bastard! He's heading for the highway. Don't lose him, sweetheart!"

Passing perilously through an intersection on a red light, Sterling screamed. A garbage truck up ahead crept into their path.

"Hang on!" she ordered, jerking the Grand Prix out of the path of the truck and narrowly missing it.

"Weeooh!" Ben hollered. "That was great, Sterling. Great driving."

"Not so great. I've lost sight of the sedan."

Frustrated, Ben searched the traffic. "There he is. He's in the east-bound lane now. Slow down."

"Slow down? What are you thinking?"

"I'm going after him," he said, pushing open the car door.

Desperate to get the guy who tried to run-down Sterling, Ben pushed his limits, beating out a quick pace on the pavement. The traffic was on his side, slowing the sedan. Finally, he caught up, and lunged onto the trunk of the car, just as the traffic broke and the car took off again.

"You're under arrest!" he called, barely hanging onto the vehicle with his fingernails. "Pull over."

Without missing a beat, the driver pulled a U-turn, nearly spilling Ben off the trunk, but he gritted his teeth and managed to hang on. "I said pull over, moron! Make it easy on yourself."

The driver acted completely oblivious to his commands, then abruptly swerved the car in a hard left, sending Ben rolling to the gravel shoulder. Sore and bruised, but nearly numb with determination, he pulled himself to his feet and picked-up the pursuit again.

"Watch out, buddy," a driver yelled at him as he raced down the middle of the road.

"Get out of the road!" yelled another.

With lungs aching for breath, Ben kept up the chase, his sight on the black sedan stretching farther and farther.

"Hey, you want a lift?" It was Sterling, slowing beside him.

"He's getting away!"

Sterling slowed to a stop on the side of the road. "Correction. He's gone. Get in."

Admitting defeat wasn't easy, but Ben shot her a shrug. "Thanks."

"Did you get a good look at him?"

"No, did you?" He could always hope.

"No. But I can guess who it was."

"Yeah, who?" Ben asked, slouching wearily back in the seat.

"Rutherford. And running into him explains the creepy feeling I've been having."

"So you think he's hanging around. Why?"

"Gees, detective, you're losing your edge. Why do you think? He has unfinished business."

Ben couldn't stifle a smile. She could be right. It made perfect sense that Jerry was lying low, but not out of the picture. Sterling's keen investigation skills had always been impressive. She was one of the best, yet she always had to keep proving it, to herself more than anyone else. "Well his wife says he didn't take any clothes on his alleged business trip, so that's a little fishy. Why would he want people to think he'd gone out of town?"

"Maybe to give himself more time. Obviously he didn't have a lot of time to make plans and cover his tracks." Sterling seemed to be driving on near automatic, her attention caught up in the case.

"Or he didn't go anywhere but six feet under."

"How do you explain that he called his secretary to tell her he'd be out of town?" Sterling searched his face.

"I don't know. Something's missing." Ben rubbed his eyes. It wasn't like him to be so dull-headed. "Did you get the plate?"

"Yes, but right now, let's just concentrate on getting you cleaned up. You've got a nasty cut or two," she said, concern knitting her brow.

CHAPTER 8

"Ouch!" Ben flinched as he sat on the sofa in Sterling's second story apartment.

"Hold still. I need to get the gravel cleaned out of these cuts or they'll get infected." She adjusted the lamp to better light the area.

"You're making a big deal about nothing," Ben protested.

"I said hold still." Sterling brushed back stray locks of his sleek dark hair from his forehead. Pausing, she drew in a deep breath and steadied herself. His closeness held her nearly captive in the powerful energy of his being, but she couldn't let it take her over. The price was too high. Trembling, she gently patted the skin dry. "There. I'll get a bandage."

Ben put a hand to her shoulder. "I don't need a bandage. It's just a scratch," he said, his voice low.

Sterling's breath was coming faster. Ben's touch sent torrents of sensations charging through her body. She had to get away, out of the draw of the powerful emotions invisibly flowing between them as strongly as the connection of the moon and the tide. Turning, she made a fatal mistake, and she knew it, but she couldn't help herself. She paused and took one look into his dark, steamy eyes. "It's more than a scratch, but whatever you say," she said, feeling her pulse race.

The ragged, raw emotion stirring in his rugged face reached a part of her that defied common sense.

"I can't help saying it, Sterling. I love you. Can you forgive me?" Ben pulled her in close.

His lips inches from hers, Sterling felt the fierceness of his passion sweep over her senses. She closed her eyes and held her breath, as Ben's mouth delicately took in her lower lip, then kissed her fully and ferociously. Warmth washed over her at the same time excitement sparked through her, insisting she surrender.

What seemed like a lifetime later, Ben released her and she breathed, a deep, soul-filling breath. It was as if standing in the embrace of Ben's arms, she was where she belonged.

Running his hands up her back, Ben took locks of Sterling's hair into his fingers, then cupped her face, just looking at her. His eyes holding hers mesmerized, she sensed the strength of his love and felt awed.

"You know I can't give you what you want," she breathed. "You deserve so much more."

"If all I can have is this moment with you, I'll be happy, in this moment."

"It's not fair to you, Ben." Sterling felt her will slipping.

Tilting his head slightly, he smiled. "Let me worry about that."

Sterling's heart melted, instinctively knowing Ben's love gave her life.

Passion crashed over her like fierce waves pounding against the seaside. Ben's mouth devoured hers, as his fingers tore at her clothing. She responded in kind and finally felt naked skin against naked skin charging her senses, drowning out the fears.

Lowering her to the plush carpeting, Ben covered her with his finely sculpted body, his kisses everywhere, driving her to unleash her control and experience the poignant beauty and bone-wrenching delight of being fully alive. Sterling moaned as his mouth moistened and caressed each breast. She wanting nothing but to touch him and take of his fire.

Her fingers kneading his firmly muscled back as he trailed kisses along her thighs, Sterling arched to him. And Ben kept going, proclaiming his love with each searing kiss to her toes, her calves, then, turning her, pressing his lips to her behind, the small of her back, and gently nuzzling her ears.

"I love you, Sterling," he breathed, once again turning her over to face him, then pulling her atop him.

Ben's eyes glazed with passion, Sterling felt taken up by their intensity. No words could express her feelings. She only knew of the emotions crashing through her. Silently, she told him, as she pressed hot kisses to his solid shoulder, his darkly matted chest, his taut abdomen, his firm thigh. Shudders rushed through him as he paused briefly for protection, then pulled her astride him again.

Close, so close she felt their hearts beating as one, she burrowed her fingers into Ben's damp, dark locks and savored the sweet momentum of their love. With his mouth clamped to hers, Sterling felt the breadth of their emotions mingling and combining as his kiss let loose her true feelings. Once loosed, they swelled like rolling ocean waves, plunging her deeply into the fierceness of their beauty. Her soul fairly singing, she gazed through heavy-lidded eyes at Ben below her. His eyes on her, their gazes collided in a final, shuddering surge.

Winded and spent, Sterling slipped to lie cozily alongside Ben's strong frame, one leg casually draped over his. He lay quietly, his chest rising and falling with the contentedness of a comfortable rest.

A glow warmed her body from head to toe. *Lying here beside him feels so right. It's as if the immenseness of our passion blots out the pain when I'm with him.*

But this was exactly what the warning flags of days ago had signaled Sterling would happen. Intuition knew the case would force her to confront her feelings. The very feelings that would lead to enormous pain. As delicious and wonderful as the feelings were, they were equally deadly because they made her vulnerable. It felt like everything she'd relied on for sanity in the last two years was crumbling away, and she didn't know if she could survive.

"Ben," she whispered. "It's time to go." It sounded so cold, incongruent with the depth of experience they'd shared. *But it's the smartest thing to do.*

Ben stirred from his shallow slumber. "Hey beautiful." His face lighted briefly by his signature smile, then he closed his eyes again.

"Get up, lazy man," Sterling chuckled, gathering her clothes. "I have things to do, remember?"

Propping himself up on one elbow, Ben gave her a devilish grin. "It seems like we just did some things. Some pretty wonderful things."

Ignoring the flutter of her heart, Sterling tossed his clothes at him. "Get up. I mean it."

Ben's eyes instantly went dark, and she turned away.

"I get it," he said, his voice flat. "The moment is over."

Delicate embers of dying hopes filled the silence between them as Ben drew on his clothes. But Sterling didn't let herself imagine other possibilities or mourn the loss. Her profession had become a comfortable companion and right now, as always, it drew her attention.

"I'll take you back to your car, then we can check out the envelope I found at Pamela's," Sterling suggested.

"Why can't we do it here?" Ben glanced around the sunny apartment. "What are you trying to pull?"

"Nothing. The envelope is in the car. Besides, I need to go over something at my office, so let's meet there. Trust me."

BEN PAUSED at the elevator long enough to see it stopped on the fourth floor. Then he took the stairs up to Sterling's office two at a time and charged through the front door.

Michelle looked up. "Detective Kirby, I'll tell Sterling."

"Don't bother," Ben barked. "She's expecting me."

He found Sterling at her desk, the manila envelope sitting in front of her. She turned startlingly innocent eyes on him.

"How did you get back here so quickly, Sterling?" he asked. Ben's heart stumbled inside his chest. Would the sight of her ever not catch his breath? "What are you up to?"

"You have such a suspicious mind, Ben."

"It comes with the job, babe. Now let me see what's in the envelope. At least what's left after you've censored it."

Composed, her expression gave up nothing, but he knew her too well.

Sterling pushed the envelope toward him. "Help yourself. And you don't have to act so wronged, detective. I didn't wait for you because I thought you were going to check out the condo after I dropped you off. You did get interrupted, remember? Change your mind?"

Ben shifted his feet, and carefully pulled out the contents. *Clearly, Sterling has the upper hand, and she knows it.* "I suspected whatever you found in this envelope would be important."

"Maybe. It appears to be very clichéd, at least." Sterling leaned back in her chair and crossed her arms, her eyes on him like hot embers.

"Compromising photos taken of a tryst between the now-deceased Pamela Witt and her lover -- Jerry Rutherford." Ben turned the photos over carefully.

"Nothing to give a clue who took the pictures. I checked," Sterling said. "Of course, they're loaded with prints, but maybe the lab could pick-up something useful. I'd be interested in knowing what you find out."

Ben slid the photos inside the envelope and looked back into Sterling's face. So much had happened between them, why couldn't he see it written on that lovely face? Something to prove their relationship had meaning. "Sure," he mumbled. "I'll call you when I get the results. But there's no mystery here, Sterling. Rutherford was somewhat of a public figure. Someone caught him with his lover and tried to profit from it. The poor sap isn't going to net much now."

"Who's the poor sap?" Sterling asked, shifting in her chair. "Maybe this case isn't as open and shut as it seems. Maybe it's all purely circumstantial."

"As far as the murder goes, my money is still on Jerry. And I'm not so sure his wife is squeaky clean, either."

Sterling's mouth dropped open. "You must be joking. You still suspect Sara?"

"She's got motive. And where is her husband, Sterling?" Ben turned toward the door, loath to leave her, but determined.

"What are you saying? That Sara killed both Pamela and Jerry? Then why did she hire Lacey and me? And who were you and I chasing this afternoon?"

Sterling followed behind him, so close the scent of her fragrance drifted through his mind, muddying his thoughts. "First of all, Sara could have hired you to throw off the investigation. She has no alibi for the time of the murder." Ben nodded to Michelle and continued toward the outside hall. "And we don't know who we were chasing. I still have to run the plates, but I'll bet you the car was a rental. Dead end."

"You're suggesting a jealous wife committed a double murder? You've seen too many cop shows, detective."

Ben stopped in the hall and turned to her. Her hands perched on slim hips, her mouth forming a perfect, determined pout, her large blue-green eyes framed with lovely dark lashes; Sterling drove all thoughts of Sara, Jerry, and Pamela out of his mind. "You know I don't watch television, Sterling."

"Sara didn't do it."

"Is there something you're holding back? Maybe something from the envelope?"

"Would I withhold evidence?" Her eyes twinkled, and Ben's heart twisted mercilessly.

"The question is, are you?"

"I've given you all the contents of the envelope. Trust me. It's just a gut instinct."

"That's what I thought." Ben tilted his head and fixed her with a stare. "I know about your gut instincts, Sterling. But I also remember the times, before you quit the force, that you put yourself in harm's way just so you could make a collar, using, by the way, information you should have shared with your commanding officer."

"I remember." Sterling's eyes dipped.

Ben shook his head and headed toward the elevator.

. . . .

"Hmm, that detective is persistent, isn't he?" Michelle gave Sterling a pointed look.

Sterling paused. "What do you mean?"

"He's been here three days in a row."

Michelle's smile spoke volumes. Sterling decided to play dumb. "He's working an investigation and the agency is involved."

"I know, but, there's more going on behind those big blue eyes than police work. When you two are in the same room, it feels like I'm standing near a geyser."

"What?"

"Yeah. It feels like something very strong is churning just below the surface, and any minute it's going to--"

"Stop." Sterling held up her hands in protest and glared at Michelle. "Just stop talking like that."

"You know I'm sensitive, Sterling. I can just feel stuff." The young woman looked up, blinking innocent eyes, but nonetheless solidly convinced. "I'm usually pretty right. There is definitely something going on between the lines. Or is it between the sheets?" Michelle's eyes now glinted brightly. A little too brightly.

Sterling straightened and put her finger to her lips. "Shh. You may have a gift, or something, but this time your sensitivities are off, sort of, so just stop talking about it. Please."

"Sure. My lips are sealed," Michelle said sweetly, but obviously she wasn't buying it.

"Okay, well, to be perfectly honest, Ben and I have history, but nothing else. Just history."

"Okay."

"So," she continued, feeling lost, "enough said, right?"

"Got it." Michelle turned her attention to the computer and turned up the music on her docked mp3 player. Birds chirping and ocean waves crashing onto a beach filled the room.

Sterling stepped into her office. She suspected Michelle really did get it, and understood even more than before the silly little conversation transpired.

Oh well, it doesn't matter. What does matter is winding up this case.

Sterling knew exactly what to do. If she could just keep her thoughts tied-up, controlled, the case would unfold, like cases always do. *It just takes a little investigation, and after all, that's what I do.*

"Michelle," she called, "Can you get me the Hansen file?"

A minute later, Sterling sorted through the file's documents. She hadn't lied to Ben. It wasn't like she was withholding evidence. He had equal opportunity to put two and two together. It just happened to be her good fortune to hold previously obtained information from a similar case she'd closed months ago.

Mr. Hansen had asked Aegar Investigations to uncover the identity of a blackmailer who'd photographed him having intimate relations with a woman other than Mrs. Hansen. If Sterling's memory proved right, similarities between photos in both cases might be the clue that would lead her to Jerry before Ben found him. It was a police investigation but it was her job to help her client. If she could find Jerry's whereabouts first, so be it.

Bingo. Holding up a photo from the Hansen file, Sterling compared it in her mind's eye with the photos she'd handed over to Ben. It was too good to be true. The similarities struck her as uncanny. It's almost as if both sets of photos had been posed for. A shiver slipped down her spine. It was eerie.

On the back she'd penned the name and address of the private detective who'd snapped the shots. *Charlie Dewberry.* She'd made it her business to delve into the comings and goings of the PI who would do that kind of dirty work. Spilling out more photos from the file, she sorted through the guy's story: too many debts at Off Track Betting; too many nights of high-stakes gambling in the back room at Pineapple's. Sterling stared at the photo she'd snapped of him and area drug kingpin Digger Johnson standing outside a warehouse located on the edge of downtown Laurelwood. That's when she'd made Dewberry's connection to the criminal element.

Setting her dark gray fedora atop her head, she grabbed her spring trenchcoat and slipped it on as she quickly walked past Michelle. She felt very Mickey Spillane.

"I'll be out this afternoon. You can reach me on my cell phone if you need me."

CHAPTER 9

*S*terling cursed under her breath. *Why do these things keep happening to me?* In the two years since she and Lacey opened their detective agency, finding bodies had not been every day fare.

But here Sterling stood, staring down at the second dead body she'd come across in three days, and the day wasn't quite yet over either.

Following her instincts, Sterling had driven to Dewberry's office in a converted old house in downtown Laurelwood. If her hunch proved correct, Dewberry had snapped the incriminating photos of Pamela and Jerry. Dewberry was one guy who did not do credit to the business. Sort of a sleazy gumshoe. Sterling had hoped to shake his chain, confident he'd spill a lead or two.

Dewberry would be of little help now, she thought ruefully. Sitting in a leather chair behind his desk, the private investigator's head slumped awkwardly to one side and his eyes looked widely vacant from inside the plastic bag covering his head. A half-eaten double cheeseburger sitting in his lap and papers strewn at his feet belied a struggle. But even though it was after-hours and the building was deserted, the office door had been standing open when she'd arrived.

A close scrutiny of the lock told Sterling there were no signs of a forced entry.

Footsteps coming down the hall sent Sterling into the adjoining room. She pulled the door nearly shut and hugged the wall, her heart pounding loudly inside her head.

Maybe her luck was changing, Sterling thought. Maybe the killer was still around. Maybe she'd have this case closed by the end of the day. Then it would be, so long Ben Kirby, not to mention a little gloating for beating him to the perp.

The steps barely paused at Dewberry's office, then traveled toward the stairs.

More good luck, she thought, noticing the sign over a door across the room reading EXIT.

Sterling crossed the room, slowly turned the knob, quietly opened the door and peeked out. The hall looked empty. Her heart raced as she scanned up and down the dimly lit corridor. Cautiously, she stepped into the hallway. Pulling her fedora down low and adjusting her coat collar closer around her neck, she walked toward the stairway, keeping a vigilant eye.

Two steps down the hall and gruffly a voice sounded behind her.

"Hold it!"

Adrenaline and self-preservation surged through Sterling's veins, compelling her steps to hasten on. Yes, she wanted this slimebag, but this was not the way she wanted it to come down. Sneaking up from behind her like this put the perp at an obvious advantage.

Suddenly, hands around her ankles yanked Sterling's feet out from under her. She fell flat onto the floor, her arms stinging as they broke her fall. Before she could gather her defenses, the harsh hands forced her over onto her back, and she stared up into the barrel of a gun.

"Hold it right there," the gunman gruffly commanded, his foot planted on her churning stomach.

"Take it easy, I'm not moving," she cried, raising her hands in surrender, but not moving her eyes from the .38 pointing at her head.

"Sterling?"

She knew that voice. "Ben?"

Instantly, he moved his foot off her and held out his hand. "Are you okay?" Ben effortlessly pulled Sterling to her feet, then shot a furtive gaze up and down her body. "Are you okay?" he asked again. "Why didn't you stop when I told you to?"

"I didn't know it was you." Sterling felt like an idiot, but tried to cover her unease, smoothing the lines of her skirt and ignoring Ben's eyes.

"What the hell are you doing here?"

"I could ask you the same question." Maybe she could distract him, deflect his accusations and suspicions.

"You're going to have a bruise here." Gently Ben touched her forehead, sending her heart tripping.

But like a flash, understanding dawned in her mind. Angrily, she pushed his hand away. "You rat! You followed me, didn't you? It was you I heard coming down the hall a few minutes ago. How did you get behind me?"

"This hall circles the floor. I was making the rounds. I thought you were the killer." Ben shoved his gun back into his underarm holster.

"But you didn't go into the office. How did you know someone had been killed?" She didn't know which was more bruised -- her forehead or her ego.

"It didn't take more than a quick look to see that guy was history, Sterling. I saw someone leave his office, and naturally presumed it was the killer leaving the scene. I didn't know it was you."

"That doesn't explain why you just happen to be here at the same time I am." Sterling pointed an accusing finger in Ben's face, wishing she didn't feel so unnerved. *God, he was exasperating!* "You followed me."

"I did not follow you. I followed a lead, just like you did. We always did think alike." A mischievous grin lit Ben's rugged face.

His smile softened her anger and, annoyingly, spurred her pulse, but she'd be damned if she'd let on. "Ben, didn't I ask you to stop referring to the past?"

His grin slipped into a frown. "Fine. Let's concentrate on the present. Where were you going when I slammed you to the floor?"

Sterling planted her hands on her hips. "Where do you think? To follow the possible killer I thought I heard walking in the hallway. You don't suspect me, do you?"

"Of course not. It was just a question."

Noting Ben's clenched jaw and furrowed brow, Sterling felt his discomfort. "You seem uptight, or something. What are you keeping from me?"

Ben shuffled from one foot to the other. "Nothing."

Shooting him a dubious scowl, Sterling pivoted and drew her attention to the scene inside the office. Concentration grew harder the closer Ben's presence drew her in. Though perhaps unconscious on his part, Ben's power over her heart remained nonetheless all the more compelling for its innocence.

Sterling gathered her determination to piece together the puzzle and close the Witt case before her heart became hopelessly entangled. There couldn't be any more letting her guard down. The intimate times she'd spent with Ben only made things worse. What had she been thinking, letting her emotions take over? It amazed her that she could make such poor choices.

Ben cleared his throat. "Okay, maybe I'm a little nervous about you wandering around when we haven't secured the scene. I'm going to make the call to the department, then I'd like to talk with you."

Sterling crouched to scrutinize, without touching, some papers lying on the floor. "You make your call. I'll just look around."

"Sterling, you leave things be until my men get here."

Sighing, Sterling straightened and shot another look at Ben. "You don't have to caution me. I know what I'm doing. You just get the cops here. It's been a long day and the sooner your men get here, the sooner I can get some of my own answers."

LACEY PERCHED on her kitchen stool and fingered the rose quartz earring dangling from her left pierced ear. She hadn't taken the earrings off since her encounter yesterday in the hospital with Nicholas. Call it superstitious, she didn't care, they had to be her lucky earrings. How else could the return of her sweet Nick be explained, she wondered.

After the doctor released Tyler from the hospital in the afternoon, Lacey had brought her son home, fixed his favorite meal-- spaghetti, corn muffins, and fresh cantaloupe -- then coaxed him with video games into an evening of sitting put. Against his protests, Lacey had ushered him off to bed early. After making sure Tyler had a night's rest in his own bed, she would be nearly ready to release her precious son back into the world again, be it with a cast from his fingers to his shoulder.

But you know concern for Tyler is not the only reason you wanted him snug in bed tonight. Nicholas promised he would be near, but when, how...Lacey's thoughts churned and stewed as she tried to logic it out.

But honestly, none of it made any sense. Not rationally. Still, Lacey knew without doubt that Nicholas had visited her in the hospital yesterday, and maybe there had been other times, too, that she had discounted. She was as sure of it as she was sure of anything, not because her head told her it was possible, though. The sweet, unshakable knowledge of Nicholas sat firmly planted in another place located in the center of her chest.

A smile started in Lacey's heart and lifted the corners of her lips. "Nicholas," she whispered, "I know you're here. I can feel you."

"Hey beautiful." The sound of his voice struck a jubilant chord in Lacey's body. As real and solid as the kitchen walls, Nicholas sat on a stool beside her. "I knew you'd figure it out."

Leaning close, he pressed a tender kiss to her lips.

Lacey felt tears welling inside her heart. "You told me you were near, I just had to believe."

Instantly on his feet, Nicholas' arms encircled her. Lacey could feel his heart beating against her trembling body.

"Don't cry, Lacey." Nicholas brushed away a tear traipsing down her cheek. "Everything's okay now."

"Longing for you has been aching inside me for so long. Now, seeing you here, really here, holding me and kissing me, my heart can't contain the joy." Lacey rested her head against Ben's solid shoulder, wanting only to have faith that this moment would never end.

"Our love is so strong. Like I told you, nothing could keep me away." Nicholas tilted her face up to his, taking her lips in a lingering, exquisite kiss.

Fairly humming like a finely-tuned motor, Lacey let the force of their love carry her to a place of gentle calm. With Nicholas' arm draped over her shoulders, she let him lead her into the living room to nestle onto the couch together.

"Just like old times." Lacey snuggled close to him, taking in his familiar scent. "Can this really be happening?"

Silently, Nicholas stroked her cheek and Lacey gazed up into his liquid-blue eyes. From his wavy, ash-blonde hair and squarely-broad shoulders beneath his red T-shirt, to his wrinkled jeans and quirky smile, this was exactly the Nicholas she remembered. How could she question the reality of this moment?

Still, there were questions.

"Why are you here?"

"You needed me, so I came." Nicholas continued to stroke her cheek, his eyes never stirring from hers.

"But I've needed you for two years. Tyler needed you, too. Why have you come to me now?"

"You called me."

"But how?" Lacey knew the questions were coming from a place inside her that was afraid to believe, afraid she'd lose him again. Or worse, discover this was all in her head.

Nicholas drew her up close to him. He felt solid, warm, real.

"It's hard to explain," he said. "But that doesn't mean it didn't happen. Don't listen to your fears, Lacey. Listen to your heart. You know our love is as real as anything that exists in this world. And that's how you called me."

The clock in the hallway struck eleven o'clock, and Lacey yawned, relaxing comfortably into the knowing of her love for Nick.

"You better get to bed, sleepyhead," he teased.

Lacey straightened. "Will you stay?"

Nicholas smiled. "Don't worry about anything, sweetie. I'll stay until you fall asleep."

"When will you be back?" Lacey felt the fears rising again.

"I'll be back tomorrow."

"How long will you stay," she said, lowering her eyes. She couldn't bear the thoughts tumbling around inside her head.

"I'll stay as long as you need me, forever if you want."

Thinking seemed to be getting her nowhere but in concentric circles, Sterling mused. The clock on her wall beat out the minutes as she thumbed through copies of the police investigative report of Pamela's death. *Nothing here pins down motive. No leads to Jerry's whereabouts.* The key remained a dead-end, and the planner had yet to yield any clues. Sterling slammed the file folder down on her desk, and walked to the window.

City lights sparkled loudly, announcing the close of another day and nagging at her in chorus with the wall clock. A third day on the case was drawing to an end with still no breaks. Each day's passing meant the trail was just that much colder, making the odds of locating the wayward Jerry just that much slimmer. It gnawed at her, like the hungry growl of an empty stomach.

It wasn't right that Sara had to suffer so much. First her husband's betrayal and then not knowing where he was or what happens next.

Interviews with neighbors at the condo and in the Rutheford neighborhood had netted Sterling nothing she hadn't already known. *Still, maybe tomorrow I'll canvas the neighborhoods again. Maybe I'll stake-out the Rutherford's home tomorrow evening. Something's got to budge.*

Sterling's thoughts twisted, and suddenly she was there again -- the days and nights following her father's death. The wretched loneliness welled inside her, clawing at her soul.

This is ridiculous. He's been dead for fourteen years. Dead and buried. Sterling brushed away a tear trailing down her cheek. Dead and buried, she thought to herself, but never vindicated. There can't be a trial or a prison sentence for a shooter who can't be found.

Balling her fists, Sterling closed her eyes and leaned weakly against the window. The coolness of the glass felt good against her hot anger.

I still don't understand, she cried silently inside her heart, calling out to the universe, justice, someone or something that could give her a reason for the injustice of losing her father; some reason that would put her suffering into a meaningful perspective. Everything could be different, if only that night had never happened.

"Keeping late hours is hard on your health, you know."

Sterling's heart jumped into her throat, and she whirled to face the familiar intruder. "Ben! What are you doing walking in on me like that?"

The sweet, half-smile popped out onto his lips, making her heart do flip-flops.

"The door was open. You really ought to consider locking it after hours, beautiful." He made himself at home on the couch, resting his head against the back cushion, and closing his eyes.

A shadow of a beard darkened his features. Relaxed, his eyes closed, Ben's face beckoned her to touch the hollow places in his cheeks and caress the furrowed spot between his eyes.

"I take it it's been a long day for you, too," she said. Knowing the warmth growing inside her, she almost felt guilty letting her eyes linger on him.

Lazily, he raised his lids. "Come sit down, you look beat." Ben motioned to the cushion beside him. "I bet you haven't eaten dinner yet, have you?"

She gave in. Her heart pounded out a staccato beat inside her chest, but as her head rested against the back of the couch, she didn't care. Sterling closed her eyes, drew in a slow, deep breath and with it came the scent of him. No exotic, expensive cologne or anything she could put a name to. Just Ben's scent. As with so many times before, it went through her like sweet medicine for her soul.

"So, what do you say, how about going with me for a nice dinner out?"

Sterling let herself enjoy the soothing effects of the nearness of Ben for another moment. He didn't even know he had this effect on her. He couldn't know. And she wouldn't tell him. That would be the in he seemed to be dying for. A little grin escaped her lips. Dying for. Funny she'd think of it like that.

"What's so funny?"

She opened her eyes and found herself looking into his: two pools of deep blue that caught her breath.

"Nothing." After all, dying was anything but funny. Ben's expression remained unchanged, but Sterling could hear his thoughts, and he clearly knew more than she wanted him to know.

"Sterling, we're so alike, you and me." His face close enough she could feel his warm breath on her skin, Ben's voice was low and throaty.

Her breathing picked up pace to match the rapid flutter of her heart. "Oh really? You think you still know me, Ben?"

"I know what makes you see red, what makes you laugh, and what touches your heart," he said, gently laying his hand on hers. "I know what makes you get up in the morning and face each day despite the gaping hole deep inside your heart. We've both known the dark side of life and it's done something to us."

His eyes wouldn't let go. She felt painfully laid open. This was forbidden territory, even for him. *No, especially for him, because he should know better.* "And how does this make us so alike?" she asked, numbness seeping through her veins.

He flinched, almost in slow motion. "Don't play dumb, Sterling."

"Then don't play psychiatrist." Gathering her senses, she slid by him and walked across the room. She didn't glance at him, but she could feel him sink. There's nothing I can do about it, she thought to herself, shoving aside the near instinctive need to comfort him. "Besides, if we're so alike, then you know what's really making me see red is the Witt case. Do you have anything for me?"

BEN PAUSED, staring at her, his eyes searching. But she'd brought up her defenses -- she was numb.

Finally he answered. "I was right about the black sedan's plates. It was a rental car rented with a fake ID. And Dewberry's office was clean."

Sterling's eyes widened. "Dewberry's office was clean? No prints?"

"Nothing."

"What about the envelope? Did you lift anything useful off that?"

"Again, nothing. That's all I've got right now. You'll have to wait for the reports if you want anything else." Why did he keep trying? Whenever he sensed her heart opening a crack, she slammed it closed in his face.

"You know what that means?" she stated, more than asked.

The tired slump of her shoulders had disappeared. Traces of sadness that moments ago had laced her voice were gone. *Not that I'm surprised. The case takes her mind to places she can_handle.* "It means I want you to close the case with your client."

Hands on her hips, Sterling chortled. "Excuse me? You want me to what?"

Ben stepped toward the door. "C'mon, I bet you haven't eaten since breakfast. Let me buy you a late dinner at that hamburger place you like... Happy's Diner. I bet they're still serving."

"Stop changing the subject. This is a break. A small break, but nonetheless, a break, a lead, a direction to follow. Dewberry's murder was a professional hit. That means Pamela and Jerry were mixed-up with some really bad guys. Did you ID the prints on the photos?"

Ben stared at her again. Her mind caught up in the case, her spirit sparked to life and fire burned hot in her eyes. She was like a wild horse captured in a corral, ready to break loose. This was Sterling. So alive and fearless. But right now, he wanted to just hold her, talk sense into her. He caught her shoulders and forced her to face him. "You said it yourself. These people are really bad. I want you to step away."

Sterling's eyes glistened. Her lips, inches from his, slowly parted and a smile appeared. "Not a chance."

CHAPTER 10

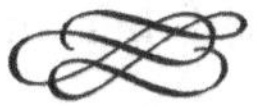

"Y ou're so stubborn!" Ben dropped his hands and shook his head.

"Maybe. But you can't seriously be suggesting I walk away from a case. It's what I do, remember? I solve cases and get paid. That's how I can pay my bills. Why can't you take my work seriously?"

Sterling stood looking up at him with those eyes the color of the Mediterranean Sea, and all he could think of was himself. How much he'd longed for her, and how much he couldn't stand it if some low-life....

"I'm waiting for your answer."

The room was closing in on him, and it felt like something had sucked all the air out. "I'm sorry, Sterling."

"That's it? That's your answer?"

Her eyes demanded the truth. "Are you really prepared to deal with the type of people involved in this case? They're probably into drug dealing, money laundering, who knows what all? Obviously killing doesn't bother them."

"They don't scare me." Sterling's chin inched up just a bit.

"I know that. And that's what scares me. A little healthy fear is good."

"That's a funny thing to hear coming out of your mouth," she said, inclining her head.

"I told you, I've changed. Why can't you see that?

"All I see is the same Ben I've always known. You're wearing a suit now, that's the only difference. You forget, I was there today when we went after the driver that tried to run us over. I saw how you take to that stuff."

Resolutely, Sterling crossed her arms over chest. Ben wasn't winning this one.

"I'm just doing my job. Yeah, maybe I get a kick out of it, but that doesn't mean I'm out of control." Ben felt an urgency to say the words so Sterling would finally get it, but by the set in her stance, he could tell he wasn't making much headway. "Could it be you see what you want to see? That way you don't have to face your own feelings."

His remark hit home, drawing her brow down. "We can't keep doing this," Sterling said.

"You're right." He dared a touch to her cheek, thinking he'd rather die than hurt her. "I guess this is hard for both of us. But I don't know what we do instead, Sterling. I don't want anything to happen to you."

"You have to let go and let me do my job."

Ben shuffled his weight from one foot to other. "Maybe so. But I don't have to like it. Truce?" he offered, knowing he wanted so much more.

Sterling closed her eyes and breathed in deeply as he waited. Was he really asking so much?

Finally, she breathed out and opened those piercingly lovely eyes. "Truce."

"Now, how about that burger?"

"You buy?"

She gave him a smile and Ben felt the air begin to move again. "I'm buying."

· · ·

Sitting comfortably across the table from him in the subdued lighting of Happy's Diner, Ben gazed at her, a twinkle shining in his eyes.

"These fries are great," he said.

Sterling nodded, her mouth full of hamburger, pickle, and lettuce. Her stomach took to the food as fast as she could put it into her mouth. Hours ago, she'd skipped lunch and dinner. A breakfast of toast and raspberry jam had left her famished long ago.

It felt good to see the shine in Ben's eyes. Since the day she ran into him at the Witt murder scene, he'd kept his eyes veiled, keeping her out. Others might not ever notice, but she recognized it. Even when they'd been intimate, the veil had remained. It was there for a reason, she knew. She'd put it there.

"So, catch me up. What's been happening in your life during the last two years? Have you been happy?"

Sterling nearly choked. *Couldn't we just stick to talking about the fries?* "Such a serious question." She eyed him over a sip from her decaf coffee. He was waiting. "You know everything. After I left the department, Lacey and I opened the agency. Work has been steady, we've been doing okay."

"Do you enjoy your work?"

Why couldn't Ben just stop aiming those eyes at her? Sterling couldn't hide from them. "I find it satisfying, yes. And it's been good for Lacey since Nicholas' death."

"Are you happy?" he persisted.

Dropping her glance to the pile of ketchup on her plate, Sterling measured her words. "Happiness isn't something I really think about."

"I see."

"Can I refill your coffee?" the waitress asked, and Sterling nodded. Ben shifted his gaze to the young woman and held out his cup.

Taking another bite from her hamburger, Sterling's mouth went dry and she could hardly taste the food that had hit the spot just moments before.

The waitress gone, Sterling swallowed hard. "What does 'I see' mean?"

Ben leaned close. "You sold out."

"Can't we just have a nice dinner without you analyzing what's wrong with me? Let's talk about something like the weather," she spouted, shifting in her seat. Her napkin fell and when she bent to pick it up, someone at the check-out caught her attention. "That's odd."

"What?" Ben turned to see the check-out.

"Don't turn around," Sterling ordered. "Something's not right."

"What do you mean?"

"The woman at the cash register is putting money from the cash drawer into what looks like a manila envelope, and the guy standing there seems, um, twitchy."

"Twitchy, as in, maybe he's sticking-up the place?" Alertness flashed in Ben's eyes, belying his calm appearance.

Ben exchanged a look with her, and Sterling knew what he had in mind.

Slowly, he eased out of the booth and sauntered the few feet to the check-out, while she sat poised, her stomach tight.

"Excuse me," she heard Ben say. "Is that a gun you're holding inside your pocket?"

Startled, the man took a step back. "Get back, I don't want to use this," he threatened, pulling out a revolver. "Now hurry up with the money!"

Sterling's attention was locked on the scene unfolding in front of her. Ben continued to walk toward the gunman, and she didn't dare aggravate the situation by stepping in too soon. *But God, the man has a gun!*

"I know you don't want any trouble." Ben's voice was smooth and commanding. "But the minute you came in here, you invited trouble. Now put down the gun."

"I told you to get back!" The man shifted his feet and shook the gun towards Ben. "Who do you think you are, Superman?"

"No, not Superman, Detective Kirby, dirt bag!"

With the mighty power and deftness of a mountain lion, Ben grabbed the nose of the revolver at the same time he kicked the man's feet out from under him. The man slammed to the floor with a loud groan, and the force of the fall sent the gun flying across the polished linoleum floor.

As startled screams filled the restaurant, Sterling jumped for the revolver, drew it up and aimed the barrel down at the man sprawled on the floor. "Freeze, scumbag."

Ben cuffed him and hauled him to his feet, while directing the cashier to call the police department.

"You sure picked the wrong day to rob this place, fool," Ben said, shoving the man into a chair. "Now sit still. I don't like having my meal interrupted. I might not hit you if you don't move a muscle."

"Detective, please, allow me to give you dinner on the house for you and your lady friend," offered the restaurant manager. "I can't thank you enough."

"That sounds like thanks enough, sir." Ben winked cheerily at Sterling.

Her heart melted. As clichéd as it was, Ben's strength and easy assuredness did something for her. It made her feel safe. Sure, she could take care of herself, but Ben made it so she didn't always have to. It felt like a luxury she'd seldom been unable to relax into since her father's death.

"What do you say, Sterling, feel like finishing our coffee?"

With the would-be robber safely stuffed inside a patrol car and on his way to be booked at the station, Sterling again gazed at Ben across the table, her senses exhilarated to match his.

"Nice job, Sterling. I knew you and I were on the same wave length."

He sent shivers running down her back with the sultry look steaming in his eyes. "All that really made your pulse rev, didn't it."

A little half-smirk lifted the corners of his lips. "Yeah. It always gives me a buzz to help out innocent people. Maybe that guy will be kept off the streets for a while, so who knows how many people we helped. And you liked it, too," he said, reaching for her hand.

Ben's touch sent her heart skipping, but Sterling steadied herself. "Yes, I liked putting him away without anyone getting hurt."

"There's more, admit it." Ben turned her hand over and peered at it, tracing the lines in her palm. "You like the risk."

"I admit I take to the challenge, but the risk, no. I do not need that adrenaline push like you do. I'm perfectly happy with my work. As dull as you think it must be, I help people, too." Her breath dragging through the pounding of her heart, Sterling pulled her hand away and tucked it under the table. "We've been all through this, Ben."

His eyes met hers, heat spilling out of them. "I just want you to be happy, and I think you sold-out on yourself. Living used to be a thrill for us. We challenged it. Now you've tried to wall up in some kind of a cocoon where you feel a degree of control over your life. You don't have to deal with complicated things like feelings." Ben lifted his coffee cup to his lips, never taking his eyes off her.

"Look, life is full of trade-offs." Sterling squirmed in her seat. "You can't tell me you haven't made any. You've made some changes. You traded-off undercover work for investigations."

Ben leaned back in his chair, contemplating. "Some trade-offs are prudent, but some are just nuts."

"You make it sound so simple. Sometimes the choice is merely the lesser of two evils." She knew exactly what he was talking about, and it bothered her. A lot.

His brow furrowed. "I didn't realize you considered me evil."

"You? Never." Sterling picked at the remains of her dinner, avoiding his eyes. Now it was clear to her why they came at each other with fists -- it made a safe boundary. Allowing emotional intimacy was acutely painful. "You are a self-indulgent, wild-hearted pest."

Ben let loose an indiscernible scoff. "Please, don't mince words. Tell me how you really feel."

Without raising her gaze, she continued, her hands fisted on the table. "And you're the most interesting, exciting, and gentle man I've ever known." Finally, she met his look.

Ben lifted an eyebrow in surprise, but she went on.

"But I can't be with you. It would be more than I could stand to get accustomed to spending all of my days and nights with you and then have to face that day."

Leaning in, he put his hand on hers. "What day, Sterling?"

His voice sounded so gentle and warm, how could she make him understand? "The day I get the call informing me of your death while performing your duty," she finished, nearly leaping from her chair. She couldn't stand the feelings threatening to tear her apart. "I have to go."

"Where are you going?"

"Home."

"I'll take you, wait," he called.

"I'll take the bus."

SHE LIED. Not about riding the bus. But when it pulled to her stop, Sterling stepped off and headed in the other direction. The last place she wanted to be was where Ben might find her.

At one a.m., the downtown Laurelwood nightspots were alive with lights and sounds. Chatter from the crowd enjoying the outdoor terrace at Johnny's filled the air. Bramole and Good Time's brimmed with friendly exchanges.

Not that it mattered. *People can party or not, it makes no difference to me.* Sterling drew the cocoon tightly about herself.

The lights and sounds of downtown faded behind her as she paced-off the blocks. Fearlessly, welcomingly, she let the darkness take her in.

A warm spring night's breeze brushed her face. Memories flooded her mind. Memories she never visited.

Another spring, another Sterling, earnestly perfecting gymnastic moves in her backyard.

"Watch me, Dad."

"I'm always watching, Sterling. Go ahead, show me your back flip."

"I did it! I really did it!"

"Way to go, Sterling. That was beautiful!"

Genuine love and pride sparkled from her father's eyes that day as he hugged her hard. It was such a simple moment in her young life, but so indicative of the many seemingly insignificant ways her father's love had fueled her spirit.

Of course, all Sterling's memories weren't cotton candy. Only vaguely aware of the blocks of darkness now between her and the activity of the downtown, she let her thoughts flow.

"Sterling, tone down that make-up. You want people to mistake you for a clown?"

"Dad, I'm going to a party. I have to wear this or I'll look like a kid."

"Sweetie, I'm sorry to break this to you, but you're still 12 years old, last time I checked. You are a kid."

"But Dad--"

"Upstairs and turn yourself back into my beautiful daughter, or you'll not leave this house."

"You don't get it!"

The memory made her smile because her dad had been right. She'd looked more like a clown, more than herself.

Her insides winced painfully.

This is ridiculous. Sterling shook her head, refusing to get sucked any further into the memories. They didn't soothe her, they only reminded her how much she hated the gunman who stole her life. The sweet, secure life of love and laughter her father had provided.

Suddenly aware she'd wandered mindlessly quite far from the downtown, Sterling glanced around the dimly lit street. A figure cloaked in the shadows behind her stopped and looked into a parked car, then turned off down an alley bordered by an abandoned building.

Feeling vulnerable with the crowds blocks away, a shudder slithered down her spine and the same creepy feeling she'd felt at the condo set off warnings in her gut.

Nonchalantly, she stepped around a building into another alley and hugged the wall. Pressed against the cool concrete blocks, Sterling's heartbeat pounded loudly inside her head as she waited. Her ears tuned to approaching footsteps, she still waited. *Is someone following me?*

Nothing but the sound of dripping water from a nearby storm sewer answered her question. Drawing a deep breath, she let it out and cautiously stepped back to the main street. Except for a passing car, the street stood empty. *That's what I get for listening to Ben and all his talk about how ruthless the perp. may be. Now I'm paranoid. I'll never accomplish anything if I don't get a grip.*

Turning back towards home, Sterling picked up her pace. The eeriness still clung to her, prickling her skin. The downtown offered small comfort to the fear twisting her insides. It wasn't logical, but it still felt very real. Whatever this thing, this feeling was, it seemed to be alerting her senses to danger.

Sterling stopped in front of a store window display, but the contents were a blur as she focused on the glass. Her heart skipped a beat. The window's reflection told her what she didn't want to know. A figure had slipped into a darkened doorway across the street and stood watching her from the shadows.

Her thoughts raced as she stood frozen to the concrete. She couldn't tell if the watcher was a man or woman. *Why would someone be following me.* Sterling's police training told her to stay in public. Her private investigator instincts prompted her to challenge the watcher, bring him or her out into the open to expose an identity.

In a flash, the decision was stolen from her as the figure stepped from the shadow and swiftly pulled a handgun from his coat, aiming it at her.

Sterling flung herself to the pavement, instinctively covering her head. From above, splintered glass rained around her.

CHAPTER 11

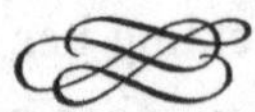

Sterling shook off pieces of glass and rose to her feet, taking only a split-second to glance around for witnesses. The evening sounds of the downtown drifted from a distance as she stood alone in the muted glow of a nearby streetlight.

Already, the figure from the shadows had a sizable lead, Sterling thought, taking off in a sprint in the direction she'd last seen the gunman. Paramount in her mind was finding the person who fired the gun at her.

Her senses tuned to any sign of the perp., Sterling heard the splash of a footstep landing in a puddle and turned down an alley in time to see the dark figure scrambling into a car.

Stop!" she demanded. "Who are you? Why were you shooting at me?"

The bright beams of the car headlights aimed at her, but Sterling stood her ground and shielded her eyes. She had to see the shooter's face. "Stop!" she cried.

Forced to jump out of the path of the careening car, Sterling chased after it for one block and then another, all the while wondering what the hell was going on. He could have taken another shot. He could have tried to run her down. Instead he ran away.

Desperately trying to get a license plate number, Sterling felt her legs giving out. *For the second time today I've missed a key figure in solving the case. The perp. was right there, steps away from me and I missed him. How could I have been so blind?*

But Sterling knew the answer to her question. With the sound of her feet slamming against the city streets, she knew her slip was the pay-off for letting Ben take her to places inside where pain engulfed her. In those throbbing places, she had no instincts, no defenses. There was no room for anything but mind-numbing loss and abandonment.

Breathless, Sterling stopped under a streetlight and leaned, tired and drained, against the pole. She was forced to accept that she had no witnesses and no clues. She'd lost the best lead yet to the Witt murder. In the darkness, the figure had slipped away as quickly as he had appeared.

LACEY PULLED the car into the drop-off zone at Laurelwood Elementary School, her stomach queasy. All the children running up to the main door seemed a little too rambunctious for her liking, considering Tyler's condition. Only a day out of the hospital, her son still seemed so fragile she wanted to wrap her arms around him and take him back to the safety of her home. Instead, she planted a kiss on his forehead as he struggled to gather up his bookbag.

"Here, let me help," she offered, but Tyler pulled away.

"It's okay, Mom, I can do it." Tyler's face screwed up in a determined scowl as he tried to manage the bag and the door alone, despite the cast on his arm.

"Okay, okay. But promise me you'll be careful and if you need help you'll ask?"

"Sure, Mom," he tossed over his shoulder and slammed the car door closed.

Lacey quickly stuck her head out the window. "I'll pick you up after school, don't forget."

"I've got soccer practice, so be here about five o'clock."

"You're not going to soccer practice, Tyler!" Lacey exclaimed. Leave it to Tyler to push to his limits.

"I'm not going to play, Mom. I'll sit out, but I have to go. I'm part of the team and I've already missed practices."

Tyler aimed innocent and sweet eyes at her and Lacey caved. "Okay. But I'm calling the coach to make sure you sit out."

"Sure, Mom."

Lacey couldn't help but linger until after Tyler had disappeared inside the school.

"He'll be fine, Lacey." It was Nicholas, sitting beside her in the car.

Lacey pulled out into the street, a smile forming on her lips. "I knew you were here."

"Good morning, sweetheart."

A luscious delight rose in her heart. "Life is so much better when you're around. What do you think of our son and his shenanigans with the swing?"

"He's a character. You're doing a great job with him, Lacey." Nicholas's face glowed, touching Lacey's soul.

"He reminds me of you," she whispered. Nicholas fingered the red curls dancing around Lacey's neck, prompting a flutter in her heart.

"He reminds me of our love."

"I can't wait for Sterling to see you," Lacey bubbled. "This will so blow her mind."

"Sterling won't see me."

Lacey took her eyes away from the moving traffic long enough to gaze at Nicholas's profile -- the wave across his forehead, the nose with a small bump on the bridge, the solid jaw -- and her heart clenched. "Why not? She loves you, too. Not like I do, but..."

"Sterling doesn't need to see me, Lacey."

Nicholas leaned over and kissed her cheek. It was such a familiar gesture, one he'd done a million times -- before he died. She breathed in deeply the serene comfort of his presence. "Is that why you didn't let Tyler see you? He doesn't need to his father?"

Nicholas stared blankly at the road ahead. "I told you, it's complicated. But in a way, yes, that's exactly why. No one but you can see me."

"So anyone who notices me talking to you right now would see that I'm talking to -- thin air?" Lacey glanced around at other drivers, suddenly feeling very self-conscious.

"Trust me, few people will notice. Everyone's too busy with their own thoughts."

"Okay. But it's too bad Lacey won't see you. She's always so certain that life is logical, that there is no magic, nothing inexplicably mysterious. I would have the last laugh, that's for certain."

THE CLOCK on the wall chimed out nine morning bells into the heavy silence.

"I'm fine, Lacey, really." Sterling glared at her sister as she continued to insist the fuss was unnecessary. "There was no need to call the police."

"I didn't actually call the police, plural. Strictly speaking, I called only one."

"I'm grateful Lacey called me," Ben said from the couch, but Sterling ignored him, directing all her attention to Lacey.

"Your first day back to work and already you're sticking your nose into places it doesn't belong." Sterling wasn't actually angry but still none too happy, either.

"What do you expect? I am a PI. Nosing around other people's business is my job, you know," Lacey retorted. "Besides, the length of your life-line is something I'm keenly interested in, little sister."

"If it had been left to you," Ben said, pointing his finger accusingly at Sterling as she finally turned to face him, "I probably wouldn't have known anything about the whole incident until after I planted flowers on your grave."

"Don't you think you're over-reacting just a bit?" Sterling shot him an impatient eye-roll. "The police were called to the scene last night, I just didn't stick around. That's one of the good things about being a PI

-- you can slip away pretty undetected. It was probably a random thing. I'm fine."

Ben had all he could do to keep from jumping off the couch. "I know you, Sterling. You went after the shooter, didn't you?"

"You wouldn't have done the same thing?" she protested, determination brightening her blue-green eyes.

Slamming his fist against the couch, Ben could hardly handle the cold fear of knowing how badly these things could go. "I'm a cop! You're not. Not anymore. You need to stop acting like one."

"What you mean is, let you beat me to the perp, let the "real" professionals take care of things for the "fake" wanna-be cop. Me."

"This isn't a game, Sterling. And it's not a competition." Ben's heart went out to Sterling, knowing her deep need like he knew his own hand; being the best was a place to hide. It kept her from having to face her pain. But right now he had to make her see the truth of the matter. He drew in a deep breath and regrouped. "So you followed the shooter, then what happened?"

"He'd already gotten a good lead while I waited for the glass to stop falling around me. I went after him, but he got the slip on me when he disappeared down an alley. Then he drove off. I couldn't catch him and I didn't get a look at him." A look of complete regret darkened Sterling's lovely face.

"He could have turned on you. You got lucky. But what about the next time? These people mean business."

"These people? You know who shot at me?" Sterling's eyes instantly glinted again with interest. "What do you know?"

"No, I don't know, but a few suspects come to mind. They must think you know something. The shooter might have been just delivering a warning. This time. These people don't miss." Ben let his head drop against the back cushion and tried to steady his breathing. Sterling had no idea the forces she was up against.

When he got Lacey's call at work this morning, Ben's knees went weak as she'd reported Sterling's brush with death the night before. It was exactly what he'd feared would happen. Sterling's involvement in the Witt case had put her in the path of a raging tornado: the turbulent cold-hearted path of a criminal.

Ben tried to swallow, but his mouth had gone dry. When the moment came, he hadn't been there to protect her. "Tell me again how it went down," he asked, trying to put the pieces together.

"The shooter followed me for a short distance first, but I didn't get much of a look," Sterling said walking from behind her desk to stand in front of him. "I would guess a medium build man, Caucasian."

Standing, Ben looked down into her resolute face and felt the familiar quiver in his stomach. She meant so much to him. How could he have let her down so? "I'm putting twenty-four hour close patrol on you until we figure out all this."

"No way! There's no justification for wasting that kind of manpower." Sterling's eyes flamed and her chin rose defiantly.

"I don't consider keeping you alive a waste of manpower."

"I don't need special attention to keep me safe. And I don't want any uniformeds getting in the way of my investigation, either."

"That's all you care about, isn't it." Ben crossed his arms over his chest. Sterling wasn't winning this one.

"Are you any different, detective?"

He looked toward Lacey sitting silently at her desk, then back to Sterling. Anger still burned in Sterling's eyes, but it didn't matter. Keeping her safe meant more to him than massaging her ego. "We're not talking about me. We're talking about you, a citizen, and your safety. I'm the cop, so what I say goes. End of discussion. I'm not leaving you uncovered. I'm not making that mistake twice."

"Ben--" she started, her eyes softening as she put her hand to his arm.

"Don't." He knew her thoughts as she knew his. She knew his remark referred to his partner's crippling accident. He knew she'd argue the differences. But death was death, no two ways about it.

Walking to the door, Ben opened it to leave. "I'm sending a patrol right over. You stay here until he arrives. Do you understand me?"

"Yes, detective," she cracked, the softness gone.

"Don't go out to get air. Don't go down the hall. Don't go to the drinking fountain. Stay here," he said, slamming his palm to the wall.

As he soundly shut the door, Ben paused, briefly, pain pounding hard inside his chest. If only Sterling could be trusted to sit tight, maybe he could keep her alive.

"You know he's only doing this because he cares about you," Lacey said. "And you're acting so defiant because you care about him."

"Thanks for the analysis, Doctor Lacey."

Lacey rolled her eyes emphatically. "It's just that I can see how right you are for each other, sis."

Sterling felt like she was being painted into a corner, and she didn't like it. "You of all people should understand. No matter how I may feel about Ben, I can't be with him."

"Me of all people?" Lacey's eyes widened.

"You know what Mom went through after Dad was killed. And I know how you've suffered since Nicholas' death." Sterling struggled with emotions welling up in her throat.

Lacey came to her, placing a gentle hand to her shoulder. "I'm sorry, Sterling. I know it was hard after Dad died. Something like that doesn't just go away. And I'll admit it has been hard with Nick being - - gone. But you've got it backwards."

"Backwards?"

"I'm the person who truly understands why you should be with Ben, no matter what."

"I don't follow," said Sterling, running her hands through her hair.

"You haven't ever heard the saying, I'd rather have been in love and lost it than never to have been in love at all?"

"I've heard something like that."

Lacey walked back to her desk and gazed softly at the snapshot of Nicholas sitting on her desk. "I know when Nicholas died you saw my grief. I would never discount the pain I've felt. God, not a day has gone by that I haven't wished he were here with me and Tyler. Still, I have wonderful memories, Sterling. Memories of loving and living and so much happiness. All of it is still alive." Turning glistening eyes on her sister, Lacey continued, passion giving life to her words. "No, I didn't get the happy-ever-after we all want. But I would never trade all the great moments with Nick, even though they were brief, in exchange for mediocre moments with someone else. Someone safe. Trust me, love never dies."

Sterling worked to swallow back the tears threatening to spill onto her cheeks, and let Lacey continue.

"Nothing in life is a sure thing. You can't isolate yourself in the hopes what happened to Mom and me won't happen to you. Gees, Sterling, you could marry an accountant and he could be strangled by reams of calculator tape or thrown out of a third story window by a disgruntled businessman."

Sterling grabbed a tissue and dabbed at her eyes. "You and Ben have something in common," she said quietly.

"Our mutual love for you?"

"Your ways of oversimplifying things."

"It is simple, sis. Maybe you need to stop thinking so much and just let it happen." Lacey's attention drew back inside, a slight smile lighting her lips.

Mulling over Lacey's words sent cold shivers through Sterling's body. It was one thing to say you believe the joy is worth the possible pain. It was quite another to live with the fear. Inside Sterling, a young voice spoke up, sounding the warning and reminding her how very large and palpable the pain felt inside her heart, and instinctively she pulled the walls of her cocoon safely around her.

The only sure thing she had going for her was her work, she told herself. It alone could be trusted to keep her at a distance from any painful emotions. If she just did her job, and did it well, everything else would be fine.

Interrupting her thoughts, Lacey spoke up. "You plan to do what Ben says, right? You're going to stay here and wait for the officer?"

Sterling leaned her elbows on the desk, resting her chin on her clasped hands. "Who do you think would want to shoot me?"

"So you believe Ben that it wasn't a random shooting?" Lacey asked, walking across the room.

"No, my instincts tell me it was deliberate. But why?"

Lacey stood in front of her, a stern, older-sisterly look darkening her face. "Ben's right. This is not something to take lightly."

"I'm not." Sterling pulled the key and Jerry's daily planner from her desk drawer. "These must have the answer to everything."

"You think somebody wants them?" Lacey picked up first the key and then flipped through the planner before handing them back to Sterling.

"That's my guess. But I've stared at them until I'm nearly blind and still I haven't figured out what's important about them." Sterling stared at the objects, willing them to spill their secrets.

"You'll get it, sis," Lacey smiled warmly down at her. "You always do. Your instincts are uncanny."

"Thanks for the pep talk, Lacey. But it doesn't change anything. Days are passing and I haven't gotten any answers for Sara. Something about this case has been gnawing at me since the first step we took inside Pamela Witt's condo. I just can't put my finger on what it is." Sterling pressed her palms against the desk. "But I'm going to figure it out if it means starting at the beginning."

"You mean Pamela's condo?"

"No, I mean the very beginning." She slipped the key and the planner inside her suit coat pocket and grabbed her car keys. "I'll be at the library."

"I knew you'd ignore Ben's instructions." Lacey turned as Sterling brushed past, but didn't try to stop her.

"He knew it too, Lacey."

"You're probably right. You two always did think alike. Which is exactly why I'm going with you." Lacey slid her purse strap over her shoulder. "I don't want to be here when he finds out you're not."

STERLING SQUIRMED and stretched her neck. Her stomach growled noisily, the sounds seemingly filling the stillness in the Laurelwood

Public Library. The emptiness in her stomach and the stiffness in her muscles told her she'd been sitting in front of the microfilm display too long, but her gut instincts told her to stay put.

"Hungry?" Lacey asked, smiling. "How about a lunch break? It's nearly two o'clock. We've been looking through these old obituaries for hours. Do you really think you're going to find something here? Why couldn't we do this on the computer back at the office?"

"I can't help but wonder if Jerry is who he says he is. I didn't have any luck online and I didn't want to ask someone with access to the police database. This is something I can't trust anybody with." Sterling answered without taking her eyes off the screen. "The best place to find out is right here." It would take amazing luck, but if one of the obituaries recorded the death of an infant who had been born on February sixth, nineteen sixty-two, Jerry's birthday, another piece of the puzzle would fall into place.

"This tedious stuff is the really fun part of being a private investigator," Lacey quipped. "But then, I don't know which I enjoy most -- the looking for a needle in a haystack part, the sitting for hours stuffed inside a car during a stake-out part, or the nearly exploding bladder part when there's no bathroom around during a surveillance. It's all such a blast."

"Are you looking through the obituaries or doing a career re-evaluation?" Sterling asked, exasperated.

"Sorry."

Suddenly, it was there. Sterling's heart stopped. "Here it is."

"What? Where?"

Pointing to the obituary listing on the screen in front of her, Sterling softly read aloud, "Rutherford, Jerald, three months. Died February sixth, nineteen sixty two."

Lacey exchanged a wide-eyed look with her. "What does this mean?"

"I don't know for sure, but you can bet this is more than an amazing coincidence."

"You were right," Lacey said, hugging her sister. "It looks like Jerry is not who he says he is." She sat back in her chair, mouth agape.

"In fact, he's been masquerading his identity for years. My guess is he assumed the dead baby's identity years before marrying Sara," Sterling said in hushed tones. The silence inside the library suddenly seemed cavernous and her words seemed to echo off the walls for any prying ears to hear.

"I guess the question is, who did he used to be?" Lacey said, twirling a strand of her curly red hair between her fingers.

"Maybe. Or maybe the question we need to answer is, why did he need a fake identity?" Sterling pulled the planner from her pocket and slowly flipped through the pages from front to back and then the reverse.

"Hmm. You know, sometimes things come together when you take a break, say, like, lunch."

Sterling chuckled at her sister's pained look of hunger. "How can you think of food when we're about to break this case?"

"It's easy. I'm not the driven half of this partnership. I need to stop by the ATM, then let's fill the void in our middles. After that, we can see where your instincts lead us. Or, we could go back to the office and rework the evidence," Lacey said, already standing with purse in hand. "Now if I can just remember my PIN. I change it often like the computer people tell you to, but then I forget it. I always need to look it up."

Only half listening, Sterling's attention focused on the planner. "You win. Lunch it is. I wouldn't want my dear sister to suffer. What the..." Sterling stopped and stared. For the first time her fingers grazed over a thickness she hadn't noticed before inside the front cover of the planner. Peering closer at the edges, she saw that the lining was rippled. How could she have missed this detail each and every time she'd inspected the object in the last few days? She peeled away the lining from the leather cover and found a credit-card size piece of plastic.

"I can't remember if it's four, two, zero, six or the other way around." Still looking for her PIN, Lacey continued. "And I'm always afraid the machine may yank away my card if I don't punch in the right numbers."

"Umm, what? Oh, your PIN. You're such a worry wart. After lunch, I'll drop you off at the office. I want to stop off at my apartment and pick up some case notes there before I run into Ben's imposed bodyguard and..." Still focusing most of her attention to the find from the dayplanner, Sterling stopped mid-sentence. "That's it!"

"Yes, I found it, but you don't have to be so happy for me." Lacey retrieved a rumpled piece of paper where she'd written her access number down. "I knew I'd find it."

"No, I'm not, I mean, I am, but that's not what I meant." Sterling's mind was abuzz. "God, I'm so stupid."

"What are you talking about?"

"This." Sterling brandished Jerry's credit card. *I knew Ben working this case would get in my way. I should never have missed this important piece.* "It was here all the time."

"A credit card? I don't get it. Does this mean we won't be going to lunch?" Lacey frowned.

Sterling's thoughts raced as she hurried her sister out the door. "This isn't a credit card, it's a memory card, and the funny looking key is a decryption key for a computer. Like you said, you have to punch in the right access code. The memory card could hold critical information Jerry needs and this key might be the way he keeps computer files secure. But without these, the information is locked, inaccessible. If my hunch is correct, Ben is right. Jerry is in deep with some very bad people. I'll explain it to you in the car."

"Remember, Ben, I'm just the messenger. You know what they say, don't kill the messenger. I just took the call."

Highly focused on teasing apart the information on the computer screen on his desk, Ben took a moment to center his attention on Jay. He hadn't heard him walk up.

"What's the message?" A sick feeling took hold in his stomach.

"The uniformed you put on Sterling said she's not in her office."

"What do you mean, she wasn't there!" Ben stormed, standing to his feet. The din inside the room suddenly grew quiet as nearly everyone's attention drew to him. "This woman's life is in danger. You tell that officer to find her," Ben directed Jay, then swept his arm around the room. "And the rest of you mind your own business."

"Take it easy, Kirby. I'm sure things aren't what they appear. It's something simple. She's probably just off visiting her nephew. Isn't he in the hospital or is he home now?"

Jay clapped his hand to Ben's shoulder, just like old times. But the gesture rang hollow and did nothing to reassure him. Ben's breath caught in his throat. He stared silently at Jay, the cold chasm between them chilling him to his bones. "You're right. Things often aren't what they appear."

"Simmer down, Kirby." Sergeant Rogard walked out of his office toward Ben. "What's going on?"

"It's pretty sad when you can't even count on fellow officers to do the one thing they're assigned to do," Ben steamed, watching Jay limp out of the room.

Sergeant Rogard eyed him knowingly. "Kirby, you're one of my best guys, but I got to tell you, I think you're taking this case too personal."

"Of course I'm taking it personal. This is my job and I'm trying to do it. Part of my job is making sure this citizen is protected."

"Citizen? You and I both know it's more than that. Sterling is your ex-girlfriend. It's not right to use this case to interfere in her life." The sergeant shook his head. "It's going to mess with your mind and you won't get the job done, Kirby. You know that."

"I worry about her, Serg. She doesn't understand what she's up against."

"This might be too hard for you. Maybe I should take you off the case."

Ben's heart nearly exploded. "No. Don't take me off this case, Serg. Not now. I'm all right. Really."

"I'm not so sure. Just get this thing over before you both get killed," he warned, sauntering back into his office.

Ben sank into the chair behind his desk, numbness seeping into his limbs. *Sterling is as bull-headed as she is beautiful. She so badly wants, no needs, to figure out this case. But how can I keep her alive long enough?*

Vulnerable with fear for Sterling, memories flooded his mind, of an eight-year-old Ben motioning his cousin to jump into the creek with him.

"Come on, Ryan, it feels great."

"I'm scared, Ben. What if my dad find's out?"

"Trust me. We'll be back at the farm before your dad gets home. He'll never know."

"Okay."

Ben ran his hands through his hair, feeling the ache of knowing he'd coaxed his cousin to make the leap that ended the boy's life. Nothing could hurt more than pulling the lifeless body from the creek and knowing it was his fault. Not the sting of the belt wielded by his uncle against his bare behind. Not the isolation he'd suffered as added penalty for disobeying. Not even the harsh words hurtled at him, telling him he didn't deserve a family that loved him because he was so vile.

Sitting up straight in his chair, the memories trickled away, and what remained was Ben's fear of causing Sterling's death. He'd led his young friend to death. He'd thrown caution to the wind and left his partner to be shot. *By God, I am not going to let it happen again.* Ben shoved his arms into his dark suit jacket, checked his duty weapon, and headed toward his car.

CHAPTER 12

Sterling opened her apartment door and froze, her breath catching in her throat as though a cold wind had nipped it.

Trembling, she walked inside, taking it all in from room to room. The navy brushed denim sofa, ripped from cushion to backrest. Her paintings, her sculpture, her kitchen cupboards, bed, and even her books -- all torn, ripped, and smashed.

Then she saw it. A small picture of her nephew taped to a wall. Horror-stricken, she plucked it off and read the note scribbled on the back: *Next time, I'll take the boy. I'll be in touch.*

Anger and fear pumped through her body, like steam in a coal-fueled locomotive, as she searched for her phone. Relieved, she pulled it intact from under a pile of pillow stuffing lying on the floor. Anxiously, she pushed the numbers to her office and waited for an answer.

"Aegar Investigation, this is Michelle, can I help you?"

"Thank God! Michelle, put Lacey on."

Seconds later Lacey chirped over the phone. "Hi sis!"

"Lacey, is there a police officer there yet?"

"Yes. He's having a cup of my specially made coffee. Why? Are you hiding?" she chuckled.

Sterling's heart clenched, unable to give the horrible news to Lacey that her beloved son may be in grave danger. She'd let her down so badly. *If I can just make this go away, maybe I can spare Lacey the anguish.* "Umm, I just wanted to make sure you're all right. Someone broke into my apartment. It looks like whoever did this was looking for something. I would guess they were looking for the key and memory card."

"Sterling, get out of there right now," Lacey demanded. "I'll call Ben."

Movement at the door captured Sterling's attention. "You don't have to." Quickly, she stuffed the note into her pocket. "He's here now. You take care of yourself, and I'll talk to you later."

"You take care of you."

Ben turned his dark eyes on her, and Sterling felt them slice her defenses, but he didn't speak a word. Silently, he surveyed the mess, and she waited, watching the small muscle in his cheek flex.

Finally, he stepped up to her and put his hand to her shoulder. "Are you hurt?"

The warmth of his hand quieted the trembling. "No. This is the way I found it when I came home. I just got here. What are you doing here?"

"I needed to talk to you and you weren't answering your cell phone. And of course, you slipped away from the close duty officer. I tried here first."

Although he didn't say the words, she could hear his unspoken accusation. "You know, you can be mad if you want, but this doesn't make you right."

"What do you mean?" Ben's eyes instantly sparked.

"I don't need police protection. I just need to finish this case," she said, knowing her voice sounded defiant.

"Can you finish the case from the morgue?" Ben picked up the phone.

"You're being ridiculous. I'm a professional. Things happen on the job and you know it." Sterling grabbed the phone away from him. "What are you doing?"

"Following police procedure, Ms. Professional Private Investigator." He pulled out his cell phone from his pocket and turned away. "I'm calling the police to the scene of a crime. You should know that like the back of your hand."

His words hurt. Sterling couldn't let them get in her way, though. "Don't patronize me." She pulled at his arm, demanding he face her.

Setting the phone down, Ben rested his hands on her shoulders. "I'm sorry. You're right, that was low. But, Sterling, this thing, this case, is plowing on like a freight train. You're standing right in the center of the tracks, and I can't do anything about it."

Staring up into his deep blue eyes, Sterling saw his anguish was real, but she couldn't help him. "I'm sorry you see it that way," she said, shirking off his touch. "I guess you don't have much faith in my ability, but you're wrong. I can take care of myself, and I can solve this case -- not from the morgue, mind you."

The phone's jangle split the heavy air filling the room.

"Ms. Aegar, I know Detective Kirby is there with you. This is Jerry Rutheford. Don't say anything to the cop and everything will be all right."

"Okay." Sterling eyed Ben as he stood watching her.

"Your sister's little boy, Tyler, is very cute and full of life. If you want him to stay that way, you'll do what I say."

Sterling's grip on the phone tightened as the man's voice stabbed her heart like cold steel. But with effort, she controlled her pain, aiming dispassionate eyes at Ben's curiosity.

"So get to the punchline. What are you selling?" she asked, trying to appease Ben's watchful interest.

"Nice job, Ms. Aegar, trying to make the cop think I'm a salesman. Now, you have something I want and I'm willing to make an exchange. You'll bring me my little black book and the key and I'll leave your darling little nephew alone."

"Sounds interesting. How do I get on board?" Sterling's heart raced nearly uncontrollably and she struggled to steady her breathing. One false move and Ben would see through her little charade. With Tyler's life on the line, she had to take orders from this slime bag, at least for now.

"Meet me at the mass transit building in thirty minutes. Alone."

Abruptly, the dial tone sounded loudly in her ear. Deliberately she replaced the receiver. Sterling couldn't avoid Ben's penetrating eyes, but would he detect the agony filling heart? *How can I pull this off? Tyler's life is in my hands.*

Resolve set in and she knew she had to make Ben believe everything was fine. *You can do this. You are going to bring this case to a close, and you don't need anyone to lead you around.* Pasting a smile to her lips, Sterling raised her eyes to meet Ben's. "Salespeople. They never know when to stop."

Ben shook his head dismissively. "I've got to call this in, Sterling, but you don't have to stick around. Why don't I take you by your office."

Sterling, don't blow this. You get only one chance. "Okay, you win. This is really giving me the creeps. My god. Some stranger comes in here and tears up my home! The sooner this case is put away the better I'll sleep. I'm not going to fight your police protection, but I can drive myself to work. You should stay here and investigate, don't you think? I don't want to get in your way." She picked up her purse and keys.

"You're right, I do need to stick around. You'll go straight to your office?" Weariness edged with tension crisped his voice.

"Scouts honor," Sterling fibbed, holding two fingers to her head. Intensely aware of the minutes ticking by, she would do whatever it took to slip out of his reach.

"Thanks for seeing it my way. This really is police business." Ben's gaze traveled up and down her suspiciously, but gave no hint of unmasking her facade.

His eyes paused on her lips, then nearly imperceptibly moved to meet her eyes. The moment hung suspended in time, and in that moment she felt her resolve weaken. It took so much effort to remain safely walled-up against the feelings that longed to pierce her defenses. For a brief second, she felt the strength of Ben and knew the relief surrendering to him would bring.

Seeming to read her thoughts, Ben inclined his head and smiled. "Are you sure you're okay, Sterling?"

Blinking, her determination revived. *Get a grip. This sinking into weakness and emotions will only get you and your loved ones hurt.*

"Yes. I'm fine," she said, clearing her throat uncomfortably. "Let me know what you find out here. You know how to reach me."

"Yes. I suppose I do."

Laden with emotion, his words nearly made her pause again. Sure she knew better than to meet a seriously bad guy alone. On the force, she would have called for backup. But she was on her own. And nothing could stop her from meeting Jerry alone before it was too late.

STERLING PUSHED OPEN the glass doors to the stately mass transit building, strolled inside, and paused beside the stairs leading to the second story. Jerry hadn't said where he'd be waiting, and with every second passing she felt the air being sucked out of her lungs.

On her way to the building, she'd placed a call to Lacey giving her the partial story. At least the part about meeting Jerry. She didn't have the heart to tell her sister about the threat to Tyler. Sterling had to make this go away without hurting Lacey. She'd weighed the options; trying to protect her sister and take care of Tyler without telling her sister could be faulty thinking. Her sister could be furious at being left out.

But when it came to it, Sterling's need to take control and shield her already hurting sister took over. With control she didn't feel, she sauntered toward a group of chairs near the bus counter, the sound of her heels striking against the stone tile floor echoed conspicuously in the spacious building.

A train from Chicago pulled up and passengers filed off. People waiting greeted the riders and made offers to carry luggage.Furtively, Sterling glanced back at the main entry doors. The large clock above the door read five-thirty, just twenty minutes had passed since the phone call that summoned her here, but it felt like a lifetime.

Sunshine filtering through the wall of windows cast radiant beams of light across the floor. It all seemed so perfectly sublime, she thought. Grandparents visiting family. College kids home for a weekend. But the fear strangling her throat reminded Sterling that the reason for being here was neither sweet nor beautiful. It was a matter of life and death.

"Have a seat, Ms. Aegar."

Sterling turned toward the voice. "Jerry Rutheford. We finally meet." Standing at her right shoulder, Jerry's pale eyes looked down into her face. His appearance matched the picture she had of him: thinning brown hair touched with gray, slim stature, thin lips, and vacant eyes.

"Have a seat, I said." Jerry motioned to a group of chairs sheltered by a large stone column and planters of dracaenas, aralia, and ficus.

Taking a seat beside him, Sterling felt keenly aware of the items inside her coat pocket. They were the keys to keeping Tyler safe, and she was not about to surrender them.

"So I assume you have my things," he said, gazing outside at the Amtrak train leaving the station.

"Did you think it would be that easy? I'd just hand them over to you?"

Jerry leaned closer, his eyes slitted and his lips twisted into a smug smile. "Yeah. You see, I know you're a smart woman, Ms. Aegar. And I know you don't want anything to happen to that sweet little boy."

"How can you guarantee me you won't hurt Tyler once you have the items?" Sterling fisted her fingers tightly. Everything was at stake and she had to keep an upper hand.

"You don't need a guarantee. You give me what belongs to me and I'll be out of here. You'll never see or hear from me again."

"Oh yeah, Jerry, or whoever you are. Why would you do that? Why should I believe you'd just be out of the picture?"

"Look," Jerry said, grabbing her arm. "You don't know what you're dealing with here. I don't want to hurt you or your nephew, but I need those numbers." Desperation and fear glowered from his eyes, and she realized this was a weak man. He was not the threat she had imagined. The threat came from someone else.

"So it's true. The memory card has information you need, like codes to access bank accounts, right? You're laundering money. Who for, drug dealers?"

"Ms. Aegar, just forget you ever saw me and give me my book and key." Jerry gritted his teeth. "I'm warning you."

"Don't threaten me, Jerry."

Suddenly Jerry stiffened, his eyes riveted to a spot past her shoulder. Turning to follow his gaze, Sterling saw a man approaching from down the hall where scents of coffee and sandwiches wafted from Corine's Café. Judging by the expensive suit the man was wearing, Sterling deduced he was higher up the hierarchy than the sap sitting beside her. "An acquaintance of yours?"

"Just keep quiet," Jerry ordered, chewing his lower lip.

"Ms. Aegar," said the man. He stepped behind her and draped his arm across her shoulder, "Rutherford. Two birds with one stone. How neat."

Sterling shirked off the man's touch. Standing to face them both, she felt a wave of revulsion wash over. These thugs, these criminals, these drug dealers were the lowest species in the food chain: people willing to feed off the weakness and suffering of other human beings. She pursed her lips and composed her thoughts. "Wow. How original. Take you all day to think of that little threat?"

"Watch your mouth, Ms. Aegar," said the man who seemed to be in the driver's seat. Looking to be in his late thirties, the man glared menacingly at her.

"Another threat, and I don't even know your name. Yet you seem to know me. I'm afraid we've never been formally introduced, but that's okay. It doesn't take a rocket scientist to recognize your kind." Sterling starred unblinking into the man's face while Jerry sat silent.

The man ran his thumb along Sterling's cheek and smirked down at her. "Pretty, smart, and spunky. Tempting combination. My name is Wade Cummings. Be assured, you won't forget it." Still holding Sterling in his gaze, Cummings questioned Jerry. "Did she give it up yet?"

Jerry stumbled nervously to his feet. "I told you I'd take care of it."

"Did she give it up?" he asked, ratcheting up his sternness.

"It's not nice to refer to me in the third person while I'm standing right here," Sterling quipped.

"That's it. Let's go." Cummings grabbed Sterling's arm and marched her toward the door.

Sterling wanted to recoil at his touch, but wouldn't give him the satisfaction.

<h1 style="text-align:center">CHAPTER 13</h1>

Something wasn't right. And it was a cinch Sterling was holding something back, thought Ben. But what the hell was it?

"Boy whoever did this sure did a number on the place," commented one of the officers collecting evidence at Sterling's apartment. "If there was something here, these perps. got it."

Ben's heart stopped beating. "Damn it. I'm such a sucker," He grabbed the phone and punched in the number for Aegar Investigations. *How could I have been so blind? Sterling has had all along what these slime bags wanted. And whatever it is, she's got it with her right now. She's so determined to solve this case, she's put her life on the line.*

The phone at Sterling's office rang one, two, three, four times. *Come on, answer the phone.*

"Aegar Investigations," answered Michelle.

"This is Detective Kirby, could I speak with Sterling?"

"I'm sorry, detective, she's not here. I haven't seen her since before lunch."

"Okay, let me speak with Lacey." A vise around his heart tightened.

"She's about to go pick-up Tyler from soccer practice. Can I take a message?"

Ben closed his eyes and tried to clear the fog that suddenly clouded his head. It could already be too late to save Sterling. "Is there still an officer guarding the office, Michelle?"

"Yes, he's sitting outside the door. Do you need to speak with him?"

"No, I'm coming right over. Tell Lacey to wait for me." Slamming down the receiver, Ben turned to the lab officer. "Are you nearly finished here?"

"Sure. Something wrong, Ben? You look like hell."

"I hate to think just how wrong things could be. I've got to split."

"Don't worry, I'll close up here. Go take care of things."

Ben took the stairs to the ground floor two at time. Sliding behind the wheel, he turned on the squad lights and squealed away from the building.

Sailing through traffic, the cars and buildings buzzed by in a blur. Ben couldn't get to Sterling fast enough. With the lead she had, he had to not only think fast, but practically read her mind.

Slamming his fist against the steering wheel, Ben couldn't stop the fears gripping his heart.

This is all my fault. If I'd kept my mind on business instead of my feelings, I'd have picked up the clues. Sterling wouldn't have slipped through my fingers. She's right, I've lost my edge.

Ben stormed through the front door at Aegar Investigations, past Michelle's stunned expression and in to confront Lacey.

"Where is she?" he demanded.

"I don't know what you're talking about."

Lacey could never tell a lie. Her face always gave her away, blushing at the slightest attempt.

"I don't have any time to play games." Ben raked his fingers through his hair, trying to rein in his emotions. "I know she has something Rutherford wants. I know she's got it with her. And what really bothers me is that whatever it is, it has something to do with the scumbags he's working for. I have to find her, Lacey, and right now."

"You know how she is, Ben. She'd kill me if I spoiled her investigation."

"You're not getting it. This isn't about Sterling's need to prove herself. This is about keeping her alive. I'm worried about her. Lacey, c'mon," he pleaded, fisting his fingers. The time for making nice was over. He had to get through to her. "We're wasting time we don't have."

Lacey blinked, twice, as realization sunk in. "Jerry's computer memory card and a key. That's what she has. I don't know all the details, but Jerry is not who he says he is. The memory card and key have something to do with bank accounts for laundering drug money. He demanded she meet him at the Laurelwood Mass Transit building. Oh God, Ben, what are we going to do?"

"We, aren't going to do anything. You are going to stay here with the officer, who will make sure you are safe. I've already sent another officer to pick up Tyler."

"Why? What's going on?" Lacey's voice seemed to stick in her throat. Her eyes went dark.

"What I've been telling your sister all along. This case involves heavy-duty low-lifes. I want Tyler secured just as a precaution."

"I can't just sit here doing nothing." Lacey's voice rose shrilly. "I should have stopped her. I should have--"

"It's not your fault, Lacey. Sterling is plenty bull-headed. I'll find her, don't worry."

LACEY WATCHED Ben rush out the door, leaving her to drop back into her chair. Tyler and Sterling were two of the most important people in the world to her, and both stood in peril right now. How could she just sit here?

Fact was, she couldn't.

Lacey reached for her car keys, her thoughts a swarm of bees.

"I know how you feel, but there is no point in taking off in a mindless search." Nick's warm hand on her shoulder stopped Lacey in her tracks.

"But Tyler is in trouble, and so is Sterling. I already lost you. I'm not going to lose another loved one, Nick. I've got to do something to help." Her heart clenched painfully as she fought a surge of panic.

Nicholas drew her to sit beside him on the couch. "Let's think about this. The police are taking care of Tyler. Ben is looking after Sterling, who, I might add, can take care of herself. Staying right here, for now, is what you can do to help."

Looking into his tender gaze, Lacey saw something that made her heartbeat quicken. "You're worried. What is it? Oh, Nick, do you know something? Is it too late? Is it Tyler?" Feeling as if she would explode with despair, Lacey searched Nick's face for answers.

"You want me to tell you that everything will be okay the way you imagine it must be and you won't suffer any more pain." Nicholas took her hands in his and held them tight. "I can't tell you what you want to hear, Lacey. Some things that happen hurt and hurt deeply. But I will tell you, you're very strong and that strength will help you no matter what happens."

All the breath in Lacey's lungs froze. She stared disbelieving into Nick's eyes. This couldn't be happening. "Is this why you're here? To help me with another death?" Lacey could barely speak.

"I told you, I'm here because of love. Nothing is more powerful, not even death." Nick put her hand to his chest and Lacey felt the beating of his heart as profoundly as though he had never left her.

Lacey felt the might of their love, overpowering the fears and leading her to grasp possibilities. Nick's presence helped calm the alarm bells clanging inside her head.

He was right. She would wait here for word and hold tight to her hope. "Stay with me?" she pleaded.

"I'll stay."

Michelle poked her head inside the door. "Are you all right, Lacey? I have a feeling something's going on. Ben stormed out of here, and…I thought I heard you talking in here?" Michelle's eyes darted around the room suspiciously.

Surprised by the intrusion, Lacey cleared her throat and shifted on the couch. "Yes, Michelle. I'm fine, but thanks for asking. I was just talking to myself. And Ben is concerned about Tyler and Sterling, but you know all about that." It was so odd to be looking right at Nick sitting beside her, his warm eyes crinkling in the corners at her uneasiness, and yet he remained invisible to Michelle. "It's late, why don't you go home?"

"You're sure you're all right, then?" Michelle's gaze continued to search the room. "I guess if there's a problem, the officer outside the door could help you. But I could stay until we hear something, if you'd like the company."

"That's very sweet and I appreciate your offer, but I'll be fine." Lacey wiggled uncomfortably, wishing Michelle would take her leave. Lying was not one of her strong suits, but she couldn't very well tell Michelle her dead husband was sitting beside her offering so much more than any degree of support anyone else could offer.

"Do you feel it?"

"Umm…feel what?" Reluctantly, Lacey crossed the room to stand at her desk and absently sort through some papers.

"There's a definite presence here. Something incredibly nice. I feel it very strongly, but then, I have psychic senses, you know."

Lacey's heart nearly dropped into her stomach. She exchanged a sly glance with Nick, who just smiled. "Well, yes, you've mentioned that before. Um, I can't explain it," she managed to blurt out.

Michelle shrugged. "Well whatever it is, it's one of those inexplicable things. Nothing to worry about. It happens to me and I just accept it." She laid a finger to her chin, puzzlement in her eyes. I don't know why I mentioned it. Anyway, good night, Lacey."

Lacey stood silent for what seemed like eons until she heard Michelle close the outer office door and head home for the evening. "Why didn't you warn me Michelle could see you?" she stormed.

"She couldn't see me." Nick stretched out on the couch, resting his head nonchalantly against the arm.

"Sorry…why didn't tell me she could sense you? If you're going to make a fool of me at least do me the courtesy of warning me." Tears breached the rims of Lacey's eyes, but she wiped them away impatiently.

Nick was off the couch in a flash, scooping up Lacey in a soft embrace. "Oh, honey. I'm so sorry, but I didn't know she would sense my presence. It was a surprise to me, too. But no harm done."

Lacey's fear and sorrow shuddered through her uncontrollably as she clung to Nicholas. "I guess I'm not ready to share you," she whimpered, barely managing all the panic rumbling in her heart.

"You don't have to."

WEAVING in and out of traffic, Ben wished he could believe his parting promise to Lacey that he would find Sterling before it was too late. Luckily, the Mass Transit building was only minutes from the Aegars' office, so at least he had a fighting chance.

Pulling into the parking lot, his breath snatched away. It was Sterling, flanked by not only the missing Rutherford, but also a known thug, walking toward a parked car.

Ben slammed the patrol car into park and slowly climbed out, determined to manage the situation without endangering Sterling's life. Something like harnessing a rodeo bull, he thought wryly.

But the men had already spied him. Brusquely, they shoved Sterling aside and bolted into their vehicle.

"Wait!" Sterling screamed. "What are you doing?"

Closing the gap between them, Ben reached for Sterling's arm and pulled her out of the path of the escaping car.

"Let me go!" Wide-eyed, she started after the car. As it sped away, Sterling stopped, breathless, and slowly turned to face him. "Do you know what you've done?"

Baffled, Ben rubbed his chin. "I don't know, maybe saved your life."

"There's no time for this. Give me your keys," she demanded, palm outstretched.

"What do you mean?"

Sterling sprinted to his car. "I've got to get to Tyler's school. Give me your keys!"

Ben's throat tightened as realization instantly set in. Sterling was acting out of fear for Tyler's life. "I'll drive. You call the school. But, Sterling, I sent a patrol officer to pick up Tyler."

"I hope the officer gets there first."

Behind the wheel again and speeding toward Tyler's school, Ben could hardly contain the contempt wrenching his gut. *How do those guys get away with wreaking havoc in the lives of good people? It's not right. God, it's not right.*

Hearing the desperation in Sterling's voice as she talked to the school secretary over her cell phone, Ben made a promise to himself: This time, Sterling and Lacey would get their happy ending.

Sterling hung up the phone and ran her hand through her dark tresses. "The school said the officer already picked up Tyler."

"Good. I'll call in an alert and we'll take over." Ben reached for the radio, but Sterling's hand stopped him.

"You can't do that."

"What are you saying?" Ben could guess what Sterling meant. Even if he didn't know her thoughts, the accusing look in her eyes gave her away.

"Haven't you already caused enough damage?"

Stiff in his seat, Ben tried to control emotions sweeping through him. "What were you doing back there, Sterling? Why can't you accept that this is a police matter? You should have told me. You should never have been there alone with those men."

"Don't you get it?" she fumed. "They'll kill Tyler if the police are involved. I want the officer to simply take him to Lacey. That's it. Then I'll wait for Rutherford's next move."

It was no use. Silently, Ben kept his eyes fixed on the road. Everything inside him longed to hold her, touch her, protect her. But as long as Sterling saw him as the enemy, they would remain worlds apart.

Blocks from the school, a patrol car parked oddly on the side of the road, its doors gaping open, caught Ben's attention at the same moment Sterling saw it.

"No, no, no!" Sterling slammed her fists against the dash.

Ben pulled his vehicle to a quick stop beside the other vehicle and ran to the open door, Sterling on his heels.

His blood going cold in his veins, Ben checked the officer who lay slumped against the steering wheel. "He's unconscious."

Sterling stared blankly up at him. "This is Tyler's back pack. We didn't get here in time, Ben. He's gone."

"Don't worry. I'll get on the radio. We'll find those bastards."

"How am I going to tell Lacey? I didn't tell her the whole story. I was trying to spare her. I thought --"

"Don't do this to yourself." Ben grasped her slim shoulders. The anguish in her face tore him open. "We'll find Tyler."

"No!" she shouted, wrenching away from his touch. "I have to do this. They'll kill him if the police are involved. I can handle it. Just take me back to my car, please. I've got to tell Lacey."

THE TRIP back to her office had been eternal. Ben hung around the sisters' office door as Sterling took a seat on the couch. She felt bitter ropes of helplessness tighten around her heart as she watched her sister sink into the couch beside her with the word of Tyler's abduction.

"I know I should have told you about the threat, but I thought I was handling it, Lacey." The words, sounding so flat and empty, fell like lifeless petals from a dying rose.

"You had good intentions, sis. I don't blame you. Everything will be okay." Lacey pulled a spring jacket from Tyler's backpack and drew it up close to her face.

Struggling with feelings of bringing this terrible thing to them, Sterling reached a comforting hand to Lacey. Although her sister seemed remarkably calm, Sterling sensed Lacey's pain. The immense hurt surged inside Sterling like an enormous ocean wave, driving her to move to a place where she could contain it. *Take charge and make things right.* "Don't worry, Lacey. I'll get him back."

"We'll get him back," Ben corrected. "This is still a police matter."

"How can you suggest that after what's happened?" Sterling charged, turning her face up to Ben. "If you hadn't interfered, I could have handled the situation."

Ben shook his head. "You're something else, you know that? If you weren't so hell-bent on doing everything yourself, maybe this could have been prevented. You interfered in an investigation."

"I'm just trying to do my job."

Ben stretched his hands out, imploring. "We're on the same side, Sterling. And we're wasting precious time. Let me call the department for help."

Sterling felt her hold on her emotions slipping, and steeled herself to Ben's frustration. Shaking and exhausted, she drew focus and stared out into the night. "No."

"Lacey? Are you going along with this madness?

Sterling couldn't face her sister's tear-weary face, but she heard her answer. "I believe in Sterling."

"Well, I think you're making a mistake. I can't force you to let me help, but you can't stop me from doing my job, either." Walking toward the door, Ben added, "You know where to find me."

Sterling choked back the urge to call out to him. Facing one of the hardest days of her life, she stood in the lonely abyss of longing to reach for help and fearing to need it.

In Ben's wake, Michelle interrupted Sterling's thoughts. "Sterling, a call for you on line one."

Reaching for her phone, Sterling stared into Lacey's sorrowful face and squared her shoulders. *No one is going to destroy my sister's happiness. I'll make sure of that.* "This is Sterling."

"Ms. Aegar, this is Cummings. You're going to get another chance to save your nephew's life. But it's up to you to cooperate. Do you intend to give me what I want?"

"Let me talk to Tyler." Sterling stood in the trembling air and shared in her sister's glimmering hope.

"Are you going to cooperate?" Sterling could see the man's gritted teeth in the persistence that sharpened his voice.

"Let me talk to Tyler," she insisted, her heart pumping like a jack-hammer inside her chest. "You're not getting anything unless I know he's all right."

Silence on the other of the line echoed in her ears for what seemed like infinite forevers. Was she blowing her only chance to save dear little Tyler?

"Hello?" Tyler's tiny voice tore at Sterling's heart.

"Tyler, it's going to be okay, sweetie."

"That's it." Only Cumming's gruffly snide voice came back to her. "Now listen to me. If you don't do exactly as I say, without the help of that cop friend of yours, that's the last time you'll ever hear your nephew's voice. Understand?"

"Completely." Numbing fingers of ice gripped Sterling's gut.

"At nine o'clock tomorrow morning, be at this phone. I'll call with instructions."

Sterling's heart clinched. "Why wait? Let's get on with it."

"Nine o'clock tomorrow morning."

The dial tone droned in her ear mercilessly. Hanging up the phone, Sterling glanced from her sister to the clock on the wall. Eight o'clock. Oceans of time stretched between her and the morning.

* * *

STILL DRESSED in her work clothes, Lacey wrapped herself in a fleece throw and leaned against Nicholas on the couch. "So Tyler's kidnapping is why you're here." She turned her face to search his for answers, fearing the worst.

"Lacey, I told you I'm here because you need me and I want to be here, especially now." Nicolas stroked her cheek and shook his head. "But I'm going to leave for a while."

Lacey stiffened. "What? Where are you going?"

He wrapped his arms tighter around her. "I'm sorry, I didn't say that very well. I'm here for you, but right now I'm going to go be with our son. I know this is hard. I can't promise everything will be as you want it but I can promise he won't be alone. And we have to trust that Sterling and Ben will do their best to bring him back safely to you."

Tears slipped down her face and Nicholas bent to kiss her. A gentle touch to her lips that quieted the fears in her chest. "Thank you. I'll be waiting. For Tyler and for you."

"I know."

CHAPTER 14

*A*fter finally convincing Lacey the best thing for her son would be for her to try to get some sleep in her own bed, Sterling sat alone in the glow of the desk lamp, the rest of the office dark and still.

With nothing but time to keep her company, thoughts sifted through her nearly always present defenses, again stirring difficult emotions.

"I can't do it, Dad."

"You're not giving up, Sterling, are you? Not my little girl."

"But I've been working on this stupid back flip for hours, days, and I still can't do it."

"What are you afraid of? That's what you need to figure out, sweetie. Then you'll do the flip."

"It's just too hard."

"Nothing is too hard for you, once you decide to do something. You can't just give up. Come on, make me proud. What are you afraid of, Sterling?"

"I don't want to do it anymore and you can't make me. I'm sick of trying. I'm not your little girl. I'm twelve years old. If you can't be proud of me even if I can't do a stupid back flip, then I don't love you anymore."

Guilt prickled Sterling's conscious and she shifted uncomfortably in her chair. She'd run away from her father that night. Hearing him calling to her to say goodbye as he went to work, she'd locked her bedroom door and refused to answer. How could she have known she'd never have another chance to tell him she loved him?

A tear drifted down her cheek and dropped onto the paper on her desk, leaving a small damp spot. The ache inside her heart grew, forcing her to make a choice: stay in the pain and ride it out or shut down.

"Mind if I come in?"

Startled, Sterling looked up to see Ben leaning casually against the doorframe. With deliberate effort, she shoved deep down the heartache echoing through her. "I didn't hear you come in."

"I knocked."

"I guess I was busy working," she offered, nervously running her hand through her hair. Feeling raw, she tried to shield her eyes from his probing look.

"Are you all right, Sterling?" Ben rounded her desk to sit on its top, too close. He stroked a lock of hair back from her face, sending her heart fluttering at the touch of his skin. His twilight-warm eyes beckoned her to trust him with her heartache. "Why are you sitting here in the darkness?"

"I've just been thinking." Ben's beard a dark stubble on his chiseled cheeks, Sterling guessed he'd put in a long day, too. "You're here on business, aren't you."

Eyeing her carefully, Ben let his hand linger on her shoulder. "I figured I'd find you here. Your apartment is a mess. You wouldn't want to bother Lacey, and you're a work-a-holic. It was an easy guess. But you haven't answered my question. Are you all right?"

Why did he have to always put her on the spot? "I'm fine. What do you want?"

Ben knew her well, at least well enough to sense she wasn't going to let him inside her deepest thoughts. His eyes went dark and he let his hand drop from her shoulder.

"I want to talk sense into you. Let me set up a tap on this phone. Let the police handle this. You can't beat these guys alone."

Sterling sat silent, listening to the muffled sounds of the street below. The immense weight of everything she'd been fighting during the last fourteen years bore ruthlessly down on her. "I am not going to let these bastards win. And I don't want you or anyone else getting in my way."

"They've contacted you, haven't they?" On his feet, Ben stared down at Sterling, daring her to hide the truth.

She couldn't look away. "Yes. They're going to call tomorrow morning with instructions for exchanging Tyler for the key and the memory card."

Ben pulled Sterling to her feet. "You've got to let me help you, Sterling. What are you afraid of?"

Stunned, Sterling felt Ben's words reverberate through her back to the time her father asked the same question. Her eyes locked to his, she stood unable to make a sound. Her knees wobbled and she struggled to make sense of the moment.

Drawing her into his arms, Ben rubbed his cheek against her hair. "You're in a pretty tough place, aren't you?"

Reluctantly resting against his solid chest, Sterling let the beating of his heart soothe her frazzled nerves.

Ben was so right, but that didn't mean she would back away. "You can stay if you want, but you have to promise to let me handle this case my way. It's the way it has to be."

"You're asking a lot, you know. It could mean my badge," he answered, still holding her close.

"It's something I have to do on my own. If anything happens and the police are responsible, well, I could never forgive myself."

"When is it going to be enough, Sterling? When are you going to stop living in the past and stop being afraid? You can't let fear shape your life." Holding her at arm's length, his eyes begged for so much more than an answer and Sterling's heart beat savagely in her chest in response.

But she couldn't muster a reasonable answer. Gathering her senses back under her reins, she stepped out of his arms. "Do we have an understanding?"

Ben ran his hand through his thick, dark locks and sighed. "God, you're a tough one. Have it your way. But I'm staying right here tonight."

EXACTLY HOW IT HAPPENED, she wasn't quite clear about, but sometime during the endless night, Sterling ended up with her head resting in Ben's lap. Rousing herself from a shallow sleep, she stretched and gazed up into his deeply blue eyes. For a moment, tenderness washed over her responding to the rich sincerity that lived there.

Then it struck her and her heart clenched. Tyler's life rested in her hands.

"I guess I dozed off," she managed. "Sorry. What time is it?" Stiff from her cramped sleep on the couch, Sterling slowly pulled herself together and withdraw from the intimate space she so readily fell into around Ben. She couldn't let anything dilute her focus.

"It's nearly eight, and there's nothing to be sorry about," Ben answered, idly scratching his head. "I dozed off, too, for a while. Got anything to eat around here?"

"There might be some crackers out there in the coffee area," Sterling motioned, stretched and walked to her desk. Eating was the last thing on her mind. Every muscle, every cell perched in anticipation of a ringing phone.

Ben, intent on making coffee, nodded to Lacey as passed him on her way through the outer office door.

Sterling's heart wrenched at the sight of Lacey's red and swollen eyes. "It's going to be all right," she assured her sister.

"I'm scared, Sterling. I just keep thinking of Tyler with those awful people." Lacey's voice broke and she sunk into the couch. She drew in a breath and let it out slowly. "But I have confidence in you. And you're right, everything will be okay."

Sterling looked at her watch, then up at the clock. Nine o'clock would come. She would deal with the creeps. Nothing could keep her from bringing Tyler back. She was a well-trained professional and she had everything to lose. That made a formidable combination that would ensure she would kick butt.

Sterling drummed her fingers nervously on the wooden desk, sounds of the coffeemaker so casually making coffee in the other room. If only she could feel more hope and less pain. It threatened to eat away at her, like a rat gnawing on a raveled piece of twine.

Without warning, Sterling caught a sense of Ben's intense presence, and she looked up to see him saunter back into her office. His eyes seized her gaze for a brief, suspended moment. Solid and assured, he not only drove her to madness, he comforted her. The thing he offered, without knowing, asked her to yield the walled-off places in her heart and soul to the gentleness of something that would sustain and fill her.

The shrill jangle of the phone sliced through the air and Sterling reached to answer it.

"Hello."

"Ms. Aegar are you ready?"

"I am." Jerry's voice made her skin crawl, but he didn't scare her. It was the other man she worried most would harm little Tyler.

"Get in your car and drive to the corner of Oak and Maple. Come alone."

There was no time for questions, with only the sound of the dial tone abruptly humming in Sterling's ear.

She steadied her racing heart with a long breath.

"I can come with you," Ben offered, regarding her with the devotion of a truly trusted friend.

"No, you can't."

His gaze never faltering told her he understood in a way only he could. "You know I'll be right here. All you have to do is call me."

• • •

Sterling parked her car in a nearly empty parking lot lined with small shops and looked around for something to clue her of her next instructions. Surely it would become obvious what she should do next. Perhaps a car would pull up beside her and one of the men would walk up.

But there was nothing. No sleazy scumbags, no Tyler, nothing glaring out a message telling her what to do.

Subtle signs of the day's beginning popped up around her as shopkeepers opened their shops for the day. The scent of baked goods wafted in through her opened window from the little bakery on the corner of the mall. It struck a surreal note in Sterling's head. Such an ordinary appearing day continued around her, yet she felt as though she stood on the brink of Hell.

A Monarch butterfly fluttered past the car window and landed on the windshield. So close to Sterling's eyes that she could see subtle variations of shades in the vivid black and orange wings, the butterfly accepted the warmth of the morning sun. With the next gentle breeze the butterfly lifted off and darted gracefully away, leaving a longing for such simple trust straining inside Sterling. The contrast between the effortless tranquility of the butterfly and the chaos Sterling faced seemed so glaringly sharp she felt it like a knife in her gut.

Doubts triggered questions. Could there be another way?

From the corner of the strip mall a faint jangle of a pay telephone sent Sterling bolting from her car and racing across the parking lot.

"I'm here," she answered, gasping.

"Do you have my articles?" Jerry asked.

"Of course. Where's my nephew?"

"Drive to the corner of Pine and Poplar. You've got ten minutes."

"Wait, I don't know if I can make it in ten minutes."

"Then you better get started, Ms. Aegar."

Leaving the phone dangling, Sterling tried to put all thoughts of what could go wrong out of her mind as she headed her car out of town toward the spot Jerry directed.

What are you afraid of Sterling? When you know the answer to that, everything will fall into place.

Her dad's words came back to her, ringing inside her head like an alarm clock. Was she making a giant mistake with Tyler's life? Sterling feared police involvement would endanger his life, but was this all just a misguided effort to prove herself? Why was that so important?

As the blocks whirred by her car window, Sterling dared herself to let the truth filter in.

What are you afraid of Sterling?

Her father's question haunted her. Why did she so fear letting Ben help? Was she afraid of letting her father down? Afraid of being less than perfect? Afraid of failure? Was she as afraid of having love as losing it? Was her fear of letting Ben close really just blocking her from making sound judgments? Too many questions and too many unknowns. *Get out of your head, Sterling. Focus.*

Sterling slowed her breathing and realized that she knew something was wrong. She'd lost control of the situation, a huge problem. They were leading her out of town and getting her alone. Shaking, Sterling grabbed her cell phone and quickly punched in the numbers to her office. With one ring, Ben was on the other end.

"What it is, Sterling?"

"I don't know, Ben. Something's not right, I can feel it. I need you with me."

"Tell me where, and I will be there."

"We've got to be discreet, you know. They're expecting me at the corner of Pine and Poplar any minute."

"Trust me. You won't see me, but I'll be there. Just in case. And if you need me to show, just whistle. You can whistle, right?"

"I can whistle." The tightness in her throat eased a bit, and she could even smile a little at his attempt to lighten up things.

"I'm on my way. And Sterling..."

"Yeah?"

"Tyler is going to be okay. I promise you. We'll handle these sleaze-bags and Tyler will be OK."

Dropping her phone to the car seat, Sterling felt the rightness of reaching out to Ben. She breathed a silent prayer. *Thanks Dad.*

Maybe she didn't know the answer to her dad's question yet, but he'd given her something to hang onto in a moment when fear nearly denied her of right-thinking.

Approaching the designated intersection, Sterling scanned the surroundings for a clue to what would happen next. Although located nearly on the outskirts of town, the area bustled with activity from shops and apartment complexes.

And this time there was no mistaking where she would find the slime bags. Her stomach tightened painfully. The sight of her nephew standing in the parking area flanked by Rutherford and Cummings was practically more than Sterling could bear.

Sterling pulled into a spillover parking lot across the street, and threw open the car door.

"Tyler!" Separating her nephew from his captors was the first order of business.

"Aunt Sterling!" Tyler tried to pull free of the man holding his small arm.

"It's all right, Tyler." Slowly approaching the group, Sterling fingered the key and memory card inside her pocket and let her strategy unfold inside of her. "Let him go, Cummings."

"Do you have my things?" the surly man hollered from across the narrow street.

"What do you think?" Longing to reach out and grab Tyler to her, Sterling knew she had to play the scum's insane game, at least a little longer.

"I think you'd better hand them over," Cummings ordered, tightening his grip on Tyler.

"Not until I know Tyler is safe." *Ben, are you here?*

"What makes you think you can order me around? You forget, we have the kid." Angrily, Cummings stepped closer, dragging Tyler with him.

Her heart pounding loudly inside her head, Sterling took a step, then another, noting the sparse traffic traveling the road. "And I have what you need to get your money. Want it?" Dangling the items in the air, Sterling lifted her fingers to her lips and let out a shrill whistle. "Then go fetch!" she hollered, pitching the key and memory card inside the dayplanner with all her might towards the road that separated her from Tyler.

"You bitch!" Cummings cursed, lunging for her as Jerry raced to the road.

"Run, Tyler, run!" Sterling screamed.

Suddenly Ben was there, breaking from behind a billboard to Sterling's right. "Here Tyler!" Ben motioned to the little boy while sprinting toward him and dodging traffic.

Tyler used Sterling's distraction to stomp on Cummings toes, break away, and run toward Ben. Frozen, Sterling watched in the split seconds it took for the two to meet. Ben protectively wrapped his arms around Tyler and pulled him to safety back on the side of the road.

Relief welled inside Sterling, blocking out all else.

Piercing pain tore at her arm. It was Cummings, wrenching her arm behind her back and pulling her across the street toward his car. Sterling's eyes locked with Ben's, his face drenched in pain and anger.

"You've got what you want, now let her go," Ben commanded, eyeing Jerry, who had avoided oncoming cars to retrieve the key, dayplanner, and memory card from the pavement and now stood back beside Cummings.

"It's not that simple, and you know it," Cummings yelled, yanking harder on Sterling's arm. "What's to say you won't come after us if I let her go?"

The smug tone of the man's voice enraged Sterling. She kicked at his shins and tried to twist free, but it only made him tug harder on her arm.

"I've got what I want. The little boy," Ben said. "You let her go and I'm through with you."

"Ha! You think I'm stupid?" Cummings growled. "Now you stay put until we're out of sight, or I'll have to do more than just yank on her arm. You understand, cop?"

Silently, Ben watched as the men shoved Sterling inside the car. She knew the helplessness he felt, as if it were her own. And though the thugs made her see red, gratitude to Ben for rescuing Tyler warmed her heart like a healing salve. *Things could have been so much worse.*

"Don't worry, Sterling. This isn't over yet," Ben called as the car drove away.

"Tyler!" Lacey opened her arms to her son as Ben brought him through the Aegar office door. "Are you all right? Did they hurt you?" she asked, taking him into her mother's embrace."I'm fine. But those men took Aunt Sterling with them."

Lacey looked up into Ben's eyes, searching. "What's happening, Ben?"

Will it never end? These sisters have been through so much. "It's true, Lacey. But I'll figure out something. Right now, you just take care of your little boy."

"I can't thank you enough." Lacy closed her eyes, hugging her son to her again.

"It wasn't me, Lacey. Sterling handled the situation just like a pro. She knew what would happen, but she did it for you and Tyler. She's very brave."

"Tyler, you go ask Michelle to get you something to eat, okay, sweetie?"

As the little boy obediently wandered out to the secretary, Lacey wrung her hands nervously. "What do we do now?"

"I want you to take your son home. I'll take care of your sister."

"But --"

"It's what she'd want you to do. No, she'd insist, Lacey. It's up to me now," Ben said, placing a reassuring hand to Lacey's shoulder.

"Okay, Ben. You're in charge. But you keep me posted, you hear?"

"You can count on it."

"And Lacey, watch your back. I can't involve the department. It's not just about police procedure or my job."

Lacey paused. Ben understood that he didn't have to say more.

"Come on, Tyler. Let's go home."

"But what about Aunt Sterling? I don't want her to be with those mean men."

"I don't either, sweetie, but Ben will take care of her."

With the sound of the door closing, Ben eased onto the couch, resting his head in his hands. Sick feelings churned inside his gut. He'd done a pretty poor job of taking care of Sterling up to now.

The look in her eyes before she disappeared seared his heart. There'd been no incrimination, no fear. In those brief moments, he'd seen only trust shining from her beautiful eyes. How could that be? It hadn't felt right from the start to ignore proper police procedure. But that was about training. Now more than ever he had to follow his gut. Trouble was, his gut was in knots.

Ben balled his fists against his brow, willing those last moments to change so he could have her safe in his arms right now. Sterling meant everything. If something happened to her, the universe might as well silence his heart.

Ancient words and ancient wounds pretzeled his insides.

"Everything you touch turns sour, Ben Kirby. How do you plan to make things right, young man?"

"I don't know, sir. Ryan was my cousin and I miss him. What can I do?"

"You can beg for forgiveness and try to live a holy life. God help you."

Too much emotion prickled inside like angry bees. Ben crossed the room and peered up into the sky, searching for relief from his agonized past.

The sunlight of earlier that morning was hidden behind gathering columns of gray clouds that threatened to soon drench the day. Watching from the window, Ben felt as helpless to control the unfolding events circling Sterling as he did to control the rising storm.

His uncle's words came back from Ben's childhood with mighty blows as usual.

Try to live a holy life. Try to live a holy life. Try to make up for the sins of my youth. It was like a bad, recurring dream. First Ryan, then Jay, now Sterling. How could he ever turn it around? Would he lose her too? The pain of it all, the existential despair that haunted him nearly made him buckle over. Unacknowledged, it robbed him of his choices, moving him to act in ways that promised him hollow absolution. Achieving high marks on the firing range, proving himself as he rose in the ranks did little to melt the shame of his imperfection, his sins. The shame persisted, as unending as the line of drug dealers, frauds, and abusers he relentlessly put in jail, trying to right the wrongs he'd committed.

But this moment thundered through him through him like nothing else, as he felt the pain. Enduring the bite of the undeserved accusations and blame incited recognition of the truth.

A ray of sunlight bursting through the clouds caught Ben's attention, drawing him to notice the sun backlighting the gray shapes in luminous splendor.

"It's not your fault, Ben Kirby. You deserve so much more than a life directed by mistaken guilt."

Like a warm breeze, Sterling's words sifted in through Ben's anguish and turmoil.

She was right. His uncle had ripped out his soul with harsh condemnations and Ben had let those hurtful beliefs ride his back all his life since. He was no more to blame for the accidental death of his cousin than he was to blame for the rain. The time had come to silence his uncle's deadly words and get on with making peace with himself.

The ache of knowing Sterling, with her gentle kindness and insight, had set him on a right path burned inside him. But more than that, Ben knew all the more keenly how incomplete he was without her.

Thoughts whirred around inside his brain like a carnival ride at the county fair. Where would Cummings have taken her? *Okay, Kirby, collect your thoughts. You know the question: What is happening right now with Sterling? Now, pull in the things you know and answer the question. That's how you'll find her.*

CHAPTER 15

*R*opes wrapped tightly around Sterling's wrists and ankles bit into her skin as she tried to wrest free. The cot she was lying on smelled of dust and cigarette smoke. The small room looked to be a storeroom, with boxes piled from floor to ceiling. The cot seemed out of place. She couldn't stop her brain from trying to imagine the cot's purpose, wondering how many people have been held here against their will. Or have its occupants been drugged-out stoolies sleeping off their latest fix, she wondered? Enough, she shouted silently to her looping thoughts. *It's time to stop theorizing and find a way out of this mess.*

In the corner of the room stood an industrial sink with one leg missing. Several thick concrete blocks propped up the missing-leg side. Alongside the sink stood a broom, mop, and pail. Not much here to work with, she thought to herself. Although she'd lost track of the time, the dusky light filtering in through a small window near the ceiling suggested the sun would be setting soon. Time was not on her side.

I don't know why they're keeping me alive. They've got what they want. Lying helplessly on the cot, anger stirred Sterling's insides.

Cummings had no sooner forced her into the back seat of the

sedan when Jerry produced the key and memory card rescued from the road where she'd thrown it. *How could I have been so stupid,* she thought, humiliation washing over her. She'd tried so hard to make her work count and to be the best she could. *And this is how it all ends, with me giving them what they need to keep right on corrupting the world, hurting people.*

But at least Tyler was safe, thanks to Ben. Visualizing Lacey reunited with her precious son right now made it all worthwhile, Sterling thought, wanting very much to be a part of the reunion and much, much more.

She and her sister not only worked together, they wanted to weave their lives together. Spring kite-flying at the park; summer picnics at the lake; autumn hikes in the mountains; winter evenings of movies and popcorn. These were the moments Sterling cherished.

And Ben. Sterling's heart clenched as in her mind's eye she saw how his quirky smile would light up his face, and felt the reality of how the briefest touch of his hand would set her heart skipping. How easily they tracked each other's thoughts, and how willingly he sought to help her. Sterling's lungs ached with a silent scream demanding she make things right.

Wriggling to sit up on the cot, Sterling searched anxiously around the room for something to free her from the ropes. Her gaze landed on the concrete blocks. Carefully standing, she hopped to the blocks and sat down against them, frantically rubbing the ropes against the coarse edge.

"C'mon," she breathed, not knowing how much time she had before someone might come in. Frantically but methodically rubbing the ropes against the roughness, Sterling felt sweat bead on her forehead. Seconds seemed to tick into hours, but finally, she broke free. Nimbly, she loosened the ropes binding her ankles.

Now what? Clearly the window would do her no good, since it was too small to crawl through. Her heartbeat pounded fiercely, as she searched the room for another way out. But footsteps sounding outside the door warned her to lie back down on the cot and hope for a miracle.

The door opened and Cummings regarded her from the doorway. Sterling glared back. "What are you going to do with me?"

Cummings ignored her question, grabbing her arm and pulling her up. "Let's go. Hey, what's going on?" His eyes flashed with surprise as he realized the ropes were gone.

Sterling's anger boiled as the man roughly drew her up close, but she kept silent.

"You were planning on leaving without saying goodbye, Sterling? I don't think so."

"Let go of me, Cummings, you pig," she demanded, trying to squirm free.

Searing pain suddenly exploded inside her head, as Cummings's fist slammed against her skull. Crumpling back onto the cot, Sterling struggled against the darkness blanking out her mind.

"When I'm done with you you'll leave," he threatened. "One way or another, I say how and I say when."

Like peering through a starless, foggy night, Sterling saw Cummings close the door behind him as she sank into the darkness.

DRESSED in a white camisole and sky-blue pajama pants dotted with fluffy, white clouds, Lacey walked into her kitchen to find Nicholas sitting at the table munching on a peach. The fresh fragrance of the ripe fruit tantalized her as she pulled up a chair opposite him and watched juice drizzle down his chin. "Mm, that peach smells good."

Nicholas swiped at his chin. "It is. Have one," he said, gesturing toward the bowl of fruit sitting on the counter. "I can't believe you found ripe peaches this early."

"It takes a bit of hunting and I pay a pretty penny, but it's an indulgence I grant myself."

Tyler was home. His incident with the kidnappers had left him shaken, but unharmed. And her beloved Nicholas was home. If her sister were safe, this moment in her kitchen would feel Sunday-afternoon sublime.

"Are you another of my indulgences, Nick?"

"I hope so." Nick winked mischievously.

Lacey's heart flip-flopped. Nick's tease felt so familiar, so like the man she'd married and shared a life with. "This moment feels very real. But how can it be real?" Her eyes dipped with the sinking question her heart.

"Don't tell me we're back to that same question. Do you want to approach it philosophically, existentially, or mystically?" Nick flashed Lacey a playful smile and poised his chin on his fingertip as though in deep thought.

"You're still teasing." Lacey bit at her lower lip, then raised her open hands to the ceiling. "God, I can't believe I'm having this discussion, much less sitting here in my kitchen with you. In the space of less than a week, my son has been hospitalized and kidnapped. My sister has been shot at and abducted. And my dead husband has suddenly reappeared. For all I know, you're a stress-induced hallucination. You know the Aegar family, we do flip out."

Nick's smile drew serious. "Wait right here," he said and left the kitchen. Seconds later he returned with a CD he popped into the player. Holding out his hand to her, Nick pulled Lacey into a gentle embrace as strains of a love song softly drifted around them.

Lacey nestled close into the warmth of Nick's neck, easily shuffling with him around the kitchen floor in time with the music. So close she could hear his breath; so close she could feel his heart steadily beating in his chest, Lacey felt transported away from her fearful reality to a place where things were as they were meant to be.

"Our love is real, Lacey. There's no need to question. You didn't just concoct me out of nothingness. You're not crazy." Nick's face nuzzled her hair, and Lacey felt the tremendous and undeniable substance of his love for her. "I'm as real as the sunshine, the rain, your breath. Just let the knowledge of us live inside you without worry or doubt. It will only grow."

Lacey wanted to believe, and knew parts of her accepted his presence as true. Now she knew her misgivings were founded not in doubt, but in self-protection. She looked up into Nick's eyes knowing she begged for something she suspected he couldn't give. "I've missed you so much," she breathed. "When you left, my heart broke. I can't go through that again."

As the song ended, a radiant silence enveloped them, punctuated by the rhythmic sing-song of crickets chirping outside the window.

Nicholas drew her face up to his. His eyes looking deeply into her eyes, he paused inches from her lips. "You have to trust me, Lacey. I didn't come back just to mess you up. Things don't work like that."

Her heart beating wildly, Lacey closed her eyes and felt Nick's lips delicately touch hers. Passion swelled inside her, as his kiss coaxed her into a swirling, mindful bliss.

"WATCH HER. I don't want any more excuses. This thing is already way out of hand."

As though she heard it from another room, Cummings's voice penetrated Sterling's consciousness. Straining to open her eyes, she felt blinding pain throbbing inside her head. It was all but more than she could bear as it nearly drowned out her memory and all her thoughts.

Then she remembered. Realization and resolve flooded her. *I'm not letting these bastards win.*

With effort, she raised her eyelids. The room spun around her. "Damn it!" she managed to exclaim, putting her hand to her head to stop the spinning.

"Don't try to move. You'll be all right if you just stay still."

Sterling focused her will and the whirling stopped. Her gaze landed on Jerry's thin face. His hollow eyes peered at her as he sat slumped in a chair near the cot. "What do you want?" she asked angrily.

"I'm making sure you don't do anything stupid again." He sighed, and continued. "You know this wouldn't be happening to you if you'd left everything alone."

"What is happening to me? And what do you mean leave things alone?" It hurt to form the sentences, but Sterling had to persevere.

Jerry nervously looked away. "I don't know what's going to happen to you. I'm just doing my job. That's all I've ever done."

"Well, not exactly all you've done," Sterling ventured. "What about Pamela? And what about Sara?"

"I didn't kill Pamela. I loved her." Jerry's pale eyes warmed for a fleeting second, then went blank again. "At least I thought I did. But I guess it was just a job for her, too."

Sterling cautiously propped herself up one elbow, hoping the room would stay still. "What do you mean?"

Jerry glanced nervously at the closed door behind him, then shrugged his shoulders. "I guess it doesn't matter. They'll probably kill you. It'll soon be over for you. You're the lucky one." His let his head sink into his outspread hands.

"What do you mean?" Sterling pressed again, ignoring his comment about her own impending death. Clearly, Jerry was having sinner's remorse and she grabbed the opportunity to learn as much as she could.

"You were right. I adopted an assumed identity years ago and I went to work for these guys. All I could think of back then was the money. They put me in the jobs I needed to be in to get them what they wanted -- turning their drug money into clean, untouchable money. They even arranged for my marriage to Sara."

"So Sara was in on the scam from the beginning?"

"No. Sara doesn't know anything. They thought it would be safer that way." Jerry turned to her, his face sorrowful with pain. "They gave me things I could never have gotten on my own."

"Even Pamela." The ugly truth was all coming into place now. Nothing in Jerry's life was real, except the pain inflicted on others.

"I thought she really cared about me. We had so much fun and I felt so alive when I was with her."

"Let me guess, you started to think you could have a real life, without the drug dealer's backing."

Silently, Jerry nodded his head.

"That's when they took the pictures of you two together, thinking they could blackmail you into staying in line."

Again, he nodded in agreement. "But I believed in our love. I told them to shove it," he said, hanging his head again.

"That's when they taught you a lesson. They not only killed her, they framed you for the murder. Then they killed Dewberry hoping to hide their connection to Pamela's murder."

"It happened too fast. I panicked. I tried to take care of things myself, because I thought if I had that money I could make a new life."

"So that plan was what I messed up for you?" Sterling choked back the sarcasm that welled in her throat. "You would be already on your way to a new life, minus your wife but with a load and a half of money?"

"It seemed like a decent plan." Jerry shook his head. "But they found me."

"Now you have to finish this job or they'll turn you over to the cops." More questions haunted her. "Was I right about the memory card?"

"Yes. I needed the memory card and the decryption key to access the hidden accounts from work. I kept the key at work. The one you found was a spare, but after the murder I couldn't go back to the bank. The key at home was the only one I could get to. And I didn't realize until it was too late that I'd inadvertently left my planner at home that morning." Jerry sighed heavily. "I'm such an idiot."

"You knew I had the book and the key, but how? A good guess?"

"No, I was watching my house, waiting for an opportunity to get the spare key and planner. When Sara wasn't around I went inside. That's when I realized you must have taken my things."

"You were following me. You saw me visit Sara." Complete realization dawned in Sterling's slightly less groggy mind. The warning flags that kept going up had everything to do with alerting her to the hidden threats around her. And nothing to do with Ben, she thought soberly. "It was you in the sedan. I don't understand why you tried to run me down in front of Pamela's condo?"

"That was really stupid." Jerry shook his head again, sadly. "I saw you go into Pamela's condo and tried to sneak in behind you. But I heard someone coming, that stupid cop, so I had to hide. I watched you and the cop. I thought…oh…I don't know if I was thinking at all. I just knew I had to get that key and the planner. And I saw you'd found the envelope of pictures. I knew if you put it all together you'd eventually connect me with the dealers. I knew I'd be finished for sure."

Sterling thought for a moment. There seemed to be so many pieces to this story, yet they all fit into one sorry life. Jerry's life of sordid ambition. "So was it you who took a shot at me the other night?"

"I didn't do that. It was Cummings. Like I said, I was trying to take care of this whole mess without them," he said, gesturing toward the other room. "But they were getting impatient for me to make the account transfers. Then they caught wind of the problems and figured out I didn't have what I needed to move the money. Cummings decided to try to scare you. He thought you'd turn the stuff over to the police and then he would have been able to get it back, from the inside. There's always somebody on the force willing to make a buck. But you don't scare easy, I guess. After Cummings tore up your apartment looking for the stuff and not finding anything, he decided to give you one more chance. He had no choice. It wasn't like anyone knew where to find what I needed. I guess someone could have tried the bank, but with the attention on me, it could have gone really bad."

Sterling stayed silent. She marveled at the workings behind the scene that kept Jerry and others like him in motion. The threats, the manipulations and deceptions that seemed so unreal yet remained very real for those involved in the crime world.

"So anyway, that's when I called you," Jerry continued. "I never really wanted to hurt you or the little boy." He slid onto the cot beside her and directed solemn eyes at her.

"What are you going to do now?" Sterling was almost beginning to feel sorry for the guy.

"I don't have any choice. I've made my bed and I have to lie in it. They've finished with me here. They'll give me another identity and I'll start up somewhere else. I've been such a damn fool. I'm just sorry I've hurt so many people. Most of all, Sara. She deserved better. She always has, I just didn't have the balls to do her right."

"It doesn't have to end like this, Jerry." Sterling slowly moved closer to him. Pain pulsed against her skull, but she strained against it. "You can salvage a life if you turn yourself in. With what you've got, you could work a deal and put these guys where they belong."

"It's no use."

"Jerry how can you say that?" she asked, shaking his shoulder. "Think of Sara. You're right, she deserves to see you, face-to-face, and hear the truth. And think of how many lives you can save just by taking these guys off the streets."

"I can't." Turning a hard, empty expression to her, Jerry pulled a gun from his pocket, and aimed it at his head. "No matter what, I'm a dead man. I've been dead for a long time, I just didn't know it."

"Jerry, no!" she screamed, wrestling with the gun.

The door blew open. "What's going on in here?" Cummings shouted.

The gun cracked, splitting the air into a million tiny pieces.

"Rutherford, you idiot! What the hell are you doing?" hollered Cummings.

Sterling didn't wait another second. Startled by the door, Jerry paused, and in that split second, Sterling gained the upper hand. Almost without effort she grabbed the gun away, then stood to face them.

"All right, hold it right there," she ordered, aiming the gun at Cummings. Her heart pumped loudly in her ears and her head throbbed, threatening to send her into a dizzy fall.

"Take it easy, Aegar." Cummings took a slow, deliberate step toward her. "Let's just think rationally about this. You're not going to pull that trigger."

"Don't test me," she threatened, circling around to the doorway. "Jerry and I are walking out of here."

Cummings chuckled. "Rutherford's not leaving. He's one of us."

Sterling swallowed hard. "Jerry, c'mon. Let's go." Sterling motioned Jerry toward the door. Staring soulfully up at her from the cot, he sat motionless, and the gravity of her situation dropped like an anvil into the pit of Sterling's stomach. She was alone.

From behind, an arm suddenly reached roughly around her neck. "Drop it," the gravelly voiced ordered.

Sterling held on, loathe to release the only leverage she had going for her.

"Hey Sterling. Now's your chance to meet the man who changed your life," Cummings boasted.

CHAPTER 16

*S*terling's mind whirled as the pain pounded. What did Cummings mean, she wondered, stunned. The gun dropped from her limp hand.

Tossing her to the cot once again, the man joined Cummings' side. "What's wrong with you, letting this little fluff of a woman get the slip on you?" he asked, roughing up Cummings's head.

"You waited long enough to help out," Cummings complained.

"I was busy."

Sterling peered up at the man. Obese, about five foot eleven, a thick shock of gray hair framed his lined and worn face. She put him at mid-fifties. He was known to law enforcement as an established criminal, drug dealer, you name it. He was one of the men pictured in the snapshot she'd taken of the now-deceased private investigator, Dewberry.

"Digger. I'm not surprised you're involved in all of this. Wherever there's stink, there's a maggot."

"Mind your mouth." Cummings threatened her with back of his hand.

"Don't worry about it," Digger mumbled. He rubbed the side of his nose with his finger and pointed low-lidded eyes at her. "But I've had more than enough of you, Ms. Aegar. You've caused more trouble than I would ever have imagined. And it will soon be over. But think of it this way. At least you're not leaving any children behind."

A coldness crept into Sterling's chest. Her gaze met the man's steely eyes and grimaced expression. Her words came out slowly. "What do you mean, exactly."

"It's sort of a long story, but I guess you deserve to hear the short version of it." Digger hauled his large body into a chair. "I was just getting the business started in town when I ran into your father, so to speak, fourteen years ago. He wouldn't come on board, so he had to go." His fingers formed the shape of a gun and Digger pointed at her. "Bang, bang."

Sterling tried to shake off the disorientation in her head, wanting to claw out the man's eyes. Gathering all her wits, she lunged for him, hatred compelling her.

"Whoa, whoa," he chuckled, as Cummings grabbed her arms, pinning them behind her back. "Something tells me you're just like your old man. Fighting for truth and justice, the whole bit. No under the table stuff for the Aegars. The whole lot of you don't understand the way things are. Not even Aegar's son-in-law had the stomach for doing business. But when I offer a cop a place on my payroll, I don't take no for an answer. Too bad your dad couldn't understand that. Too bad your brother-in-law didn't learn from it." Digger shrugged nonchalantly.

As he laid out the awful truth in front of her, the man's eyes gleamed like a Cheshire cat's in the night.

Feeling as though she'd just been punched in the gut, Sterling swallowed hard, fighting the rising nausea. "You're telling me you killed both my dad and Lacey's husband?"

"No, no. Just your old man. Cummings here popped your brother-in-law. I'm getting too old for that kind of stuff." The man's grimace widened, exposing yellow, candy-corn teeth.

"You're a liar," Sterling charged. "You're trying to mess with my mind. Nicholas was killed in a traffic stop gone bad."

"That's what the official report said. But hey, they don't call us professionals for nothing." Digger cackled again. "Just like I said, no one turns down an offer from me to do business together. And you, you should have kept your nose out of my business. But I guess stubbornness runs in your blood. Okay, enough of the history lesson. Come on Rutherford. We've got to be somewhere. Cummings, take care of her."

"You'll never get away with this," Sterling hollered, as the man headed out the door. Cummings grabbed her arm and pulled her to her feet, sending the room spinning again.

"Looks like I already have." Digger turned back to Sterling and shot her a self-satisfied grin.

"That's where you're wrong, scumbag." It was Ben. He stood straddle-legged, his .38 pointed at Digger's head. "Let her go, chump," he ordered Cummings.

Sterling's heart raced, as much in elation at seeing Ben's face as in fear for his life. The cloud of wooziness subsided as hope took hold.

Cummings snickered, provoking Sterling's stomach to churn viciously. "I guess we have a stand-off here. Question is, whose trigger is fastest?"

"Shut up!" Ben stepped closer, keeping his aim tight on Digger. "You really want to find out? Or maybe you'd just like to face the witness to Pamela's murder."

"You don't have any witness," Cummings argued.

Ben whistled shrilly and the German shepherd came charging in. Instantly, Joe started barking and growling at Cummings' leg as though he'd just cornered a choice prey.

Cummings's breath was coming hard and fast beside her ear. Sterling instinctively knew it was now or never. She grabbed her chance. "Ben, now!" she shouted as she simultaneously slammed her foot down hard on Cummings's foot, then wrenched herself free. The gun in Cumming's hand went flying across the room, clattering on the cement floor.

"You bitch!" Cummings recovered quickly and laid a violent kick to Joe's head, sending him into a whimpering puddle. The desperate man dashed to reach the gun, as Ben drove an explosive blow to

Digger's head. The large man fell into a fat lump on the floor -- out cold.

Cummings's fingers clawed at the floor, inches from the gun, as Sterling threw herself on top of him.

"Give it up," she cried, her fists pummeling his head.

"Get off me!" the man hollered, knocking Sterling off and pulling the gun into his grasp. Still lying on the cement, Cummings took calculated aim at her head. "Hold it Kirby. I told you, Sterling, you'd never forget my name. Sure, Digger took care of your old man. But if it weren't for me knocking-off your sister's husband, your life probably would have gone on just the way it was. You being a cop, chasing Daddy's shadow. And who knows what else you might have done?"

Silently, Sterling watched Cummings rise and take tentative steps toward the door. His words fell on her like rocks dropping down the side of a mountain, changing the landscape in their trail. As though holding her breath could make time stand still, Sterling watched the past and present converge. How odd, she thought, that this evil duo had dropped into her life fourteen years ago, forever changing her path. And the ripples they'd sent out still forged on, leaving destruction in their wake.

Sterling took in Ben. Standing with his gun raised ready to intervene, his face was a picture of brutal anger and hopeless frustration. Her heart smarted for him.

Breathing deeply, she glanced briefly at Jerry's nervous stare, then moved her gaze back to face Cummings' icy glare.

"Go ahead. Shoot. Shoot, you bastard!" Fury and determination raged through her and Sterling threw herself at Cummings.

As though on cue, Ben made his move as she did, kicking Cummings and knocking him to his knees. Again the gun went flying, skirting across the floor to stop in front of Jerry's feet.

"It's over, Cummings," Ben shouted, his gun at the man's temple.

"Rutherford, c'mon. We still have a chance," cried Cummings.

Sterling's heart hammered as she watched Jerry bend over slowly and pick up the gun.

"That's right, Rutherford," Cummings urged. "Let me go, cop, or he'll take out the lady."

An unearthly silence filled the room. Sterling's gaze locked with Jerry's sad eyes. Oceans of time lapsed in a split-second.

"Here," Jerry said, relinquishing the gun over to Sterling. "I've had enough."

"I don't think so, Rutherford." From the darkness in the outer room, a man emerged. "This isn't something you just quit. Now, hand over the gun, Rutherford. You too, Ben."

Sterling's heart plummeted. She wanted to scream out and that the same time shield Ben from this moment.

"Jay." Ben's voice was flat and his arm dropped to his side. "I didn't want to believe it. You gave hints, like knowing about Lacey's son being in the hospital when I hadn't said anything to you. But I didn't want to believe it."

Jay let out a hard laugh. "You never suspected anything, you were so deep into remorse. But look," he said, jumping from one foot to another. "I'm limp free. It's a miracle!"

"You let him believe he'd ruined your life! You're such a snake." Lacey shook her head in amazement. "You were best friends, partners. Why?"

"I had a better offer. I needed an excuse to slip into the shadows. It was all arranged, everything, right down to the doctor and the desk job."

Jay's smug face made Lacey's stomach lurch. She looked at Ben and saw the incredible fury harden his face.

"A perfect spot to keep informed. So what now, Jay? You kill us and just go back to doing these lowlifes' dirty work?" Ben's voice strained to understand. "What happened to you? I know you. You're better than this."

"No, you've got that wrong. You always have. This is exactly who I am." Jay spread out his arms wide. "I see an opportunity and I take it."

"All right, enough of this touchy, feely stuff." Cummings grabbed the gun out of Sterling's hand and took her arm. He gave a look toward where Digger still lay, then nodded to Jay. "He's out. Get some water to throw on him. He won't like it but we've got to get out of here."

Sterling exchanged a look with Ben. Resolve and determination formed his expression. She knew what to do.

"You're not going anywhere." Sterling slammed her heel into Cummings crotch, sending him hollering to the floor. Instantly securing the gun from Cummings, Sterling tossed it to Ben, then nailed the balled man with a hard blow to his jaw. "Shut up!"

As in synchrony with Sterling, Ben raised his gun, pointing it at his ex-partner.

"What? You're going shoot me, Ben?" Viciously, Jay pummeled Ben with words. "How could you live with yourself? Haven't you already hurt enough people? This is your chance to make something of yourself. We can be partners again and make some serious dough. That's where the power is. You don't think these guys mean anything, do you? If you want to change the world you've got to think big, higher up. I can put you where you can really do something."

At Ben's silence, Jay took a tentative step toward the door. "Rutherford, let's go."

Jerry stood suspended, seemingly unsure he should stay but not convinced he could get away with leaving, either.

Sterling held her breath. Not one of these men would get past her. She would never let any of them escape. And she knew Ben couldn't let that happen either.

"You can't leave me here." Cummings moaned, still clutching his crotch.

"Nobody's leaving." Ben's muscles rigid and his voice low, he kept his gun sighted on Jay. "Throw me your gun, Jay. It's over."

"You're wrong, Ben. I am leaving and you're not going to stop me. There's too much good times between us." Jay glanced at Sterling, at Cummings, at Rutherford, then down at Digger. Taking another step toward the door, Jay smiled at Ben. "I had you pegged all along. You always do the right thing," he shrugged. "So predictable."

As Jay turned to walk through the doorway to the outer room,

Sterling stood her ground above Cummings. Her hatred for the men -- Digger, Cummings, and now Jay -- burned in her throat. "Ben?"

"Let him go, Sterling."

Coiled for action but bone weary, Sterling felt the next move before it happened.

Ben put his lips together and whistled shrilly. "Joe, get him."

Jumping to life from nowhere, Joe sprang into action, chasing after Jay. "Get off me, you mutt!"

The sound of the gun echoed savagely through the outer warehouse and Sterling screamed as Ben ran into the next room. The sounds of scuffling rattled her nerves further, but she didn't let on.

"Don't move any of your ugly muscles, Cummings," she ordered. "You either, Rutherford." The fear of what may have happened to Ben trigged a familiar numbness. Sterling's heart began to chill, but she held fast, defying the ancient pattern of protecting herself. "Ben," she called, begging the unknown to prove her wrong -- that Ben and Joe were safe.

"It's okay here, Sterling," Ben called out. "The gun went off and hit Jay, but he'll live. Joe's a little roughed up, but he's fine, too. You okay?"

"Yeah." Daring to feel more than she had in a long time, Sterling noticed a different and satisfying sense of control take root. "I got everything here covered."

HER BREATH RACING, Sterling helped Ben restrain the four men. A certain sense of knowing began sifting into her mind and soul, speaking of resting old wounds and daring to live.

"Poor Joe," she cooed, coaxing him to lie still. "You did a great job of nailing the bastards. But we'll take care of things now. You just take it easy, fella."

With the three men safely restrained and reinforcements on the way, Ben strode to Sterling's side and pulled her close. "Thank God you're safe," he breathed. "We need to get you checked out. I'm taking you to the emergency room."

"I'm fine." Sterling was only barely aware of the throbbing inside her head.

"I mean it," he argued, his arms still tight around her. "For once, just do what I say."

She couldn't help it. The strength of Ben's arms around her anchored her and rested her thrumming pulse. Digger, Rutherford, Cummings, Jay -- they all faded into shadows as police officers led them off to squad cars and drove away. Only the warmth of Ben's embrace seemed real. "How did you know? How did you know where to find me?"

Ben winked and flashed an enchanting smile. "Our thoughts always run in the same patterns, don't they? I just followed the trail to you."

"Ben Kirby, don't think for one minute that that explanation will suffice!" Sterling pulled away, demanding an explanation.

"It was a hunch. I knew this warehouse was one of Digger's hangouts. I've heard stories of cops finding unsuspecting druggies and the like here, so it seemed a likely place for him to stash you until he could do his business. I knew he'd be eager to get his money, and he'd deal with you later. So I picked up Joe from my apartment and got over here as fast as I could. I knew if Joe saw the guy who killed Pamela, he'd go after him. Maybe that's not the same thing as an eye-witness, but it works for me."

"That's it? A lucky hunch?" Sterling teased.

"You know, sometimes a hunch is too solid to ignore. But let's talk about it later. Right now, I just want to hold you," he said, pulling her back in close to his heart.

Sterling didn't resist. She had to admit, feeling Ben's arms around her was all she really wanted right now.

BEN SAT STIFFLY on the edge of the couch at Aegar Investigation, drumming his fingers against the armrest. Sterling glanced over at him, then at Lacey sitting at her desk pulling a fresh peach from a paper bag. Finally her gaze rested on Sara sitting in the chair in front of her desk. She was the picture of composure.

"Sara, thanks for coming over so quickly. I know it's late. As the police have already informed you, Jerry is in custody. He's not guilty of Pamela's murder, but he will be charged with money laundering and fraud, among other things. He'll be facing a stiff penalty. He might be able to work out a deal, though, so you two could have a second chance. If you want it. It would be a fresh start because he's not who he has pretended to be all along." Sterling ran her hand through her hair, careful of the tender knot on her head. The day was wearing long on her shoulders, but she felt energized and alive.

Sara continued to sit motionless, her eyes barely flickering with the news. "So you're saying my husband is not the man I thought he was, in any way." Sara's tone was flat, emotionless.

"No, he isn't. You were right to think he'd married you for convenience. But it wasn't for money, as you suspected. It was for the status and position you offered. It gave him access to a life that made it easy it do whatever the drug dealers wanted from him." Sterling knew she couldn't begin to understand the turmoil this poor woman must be feeling. But she also knew, perhaps for the first time in her life, that the moment everything familiar falls apart is also the moment of most promise.

"What Sterling is telling you is right," added Ben. "Jerry assumed an entire life, set up by the criminals, simply to make money. Lots of money."

Finally, Sara crumpled. "I haven't been completely honest. The morning of the murder, I heard Jerry on the phone with that woman. I knew he was going to see her, but I didn't want to tell anyone about the call. I don't know why. I guess I just wanted my life back. I didn't care that she'd been killed."

"It's okay, Sara," Lacey comforted. "It doesn't change anything."

Sterling exchanged a knowing glance with Ben as things clicked further into place. This little deception accounted for Ben's suspicions about Sara. His instincts had picked up on her lie and naturally attributed it to guilt.

Sara blew her nose, then continued. "I suspected something was amiss with Jerry. I had for years. The trips, the evasiveness. Then when I suspected he was having an affair, I thought that might have been the reason for all the distance between us. But I always suspected it was more, and I was too afraid to change anything. As empty as it was, at least I had a marriage, and that was all I had. I blamed Pamela for ruining everything, but I was wrong. There was nothing to ruin. What kind of a person am I?"

Lacey went to Sara's side as Sterling sat watching and thinking.

"You were used, Sara. Feel angry about that. The truth can be hard, but it can also set you free. You've got another chance, now. You can start over and create a much better life for yourself."

Sterling reached for another tissue and offered it to Sara. "Lacey's right, Sara. Now's your chance to make the life you really want. One that is full and satisfying."

Sara shook her blonde hair out of her eyes and stood. "I know you're right. I always thought things would be different, but I was fooling myself. The life went out of me along with the hopes and dreams of my empty marriage. Now I'll have to figure out how to get on with living. Thank you, all of you."

As Sterling shook Sara's hand, she looked into her eyes and saw a new strength sparkling to life. "You're going to be okay, Sara."

"I suppose so. I know the truth, the whole truth. It's the thing that will set me free from loneliness. You've given me another chance for happiness," she said, hugging Lacey. "It's not going to be easy, but I want to start over. It's time."

"You're very brave. Good-luck, Sara." Sterling led Sara out the door and wished her well. As she walked back to her desk, Sterling felt strain weighing on Ben's shoulders as keenly as she felt the relief of successfully closing a case. "So, that's over."

"Who would have guessed that taking this case would lead to uncovering not only Dad's killer, but Nick's as well?" Lacey mused. "Good job, Sterling."

"It must be pretty gratifying for both of you. After all these years, you've closed the case on Joshua Aegar's murder," Ben added, gazing steadily at the floor.

"It feels pretty good. Finally justice is satisfied." Release rang inside Sterling's heart and thoughts of her father settled warmly inside her mind. The memories of her father and his love could bring her comfort and cheer now, rather than taunt her with unbearable loss.

Her eyes on Ben, Sterling's heart pounded as she watched him stand to leave.

"Well, I guess I'll get back to work. I've got things to tie up." He stretched his tall frame upward and headed toward the door, still avoiding Sterling's eyes.

"Not so fast, detective." Sterling quickly moved in front of him and pointed her finger into his chest. "You were wrong. I was right. Admit it."

"What are you talking about?" Ben stopped and gazed down at her, his eyes widening.

"I think I'll go talk to Michelle, or something." Lacey chuckled, picked up her peach and took a bite as she walked to the outer room.

"You kept insisting Sara was involved in the crimes, and you were wrong." Sterling flashed a mischievous smile up at Ben, determined to shake him up.

He shifted his weight from one foot to the other. "Yeah, yeah. I was wrong. You were right. You did a good job. I'm proud of your skills, Sterling. You've always been good. Your father would be so proud." Unabashed tenderness and respect glistened in his deep blue eyes. "And your work as a PI. is truly worthy. There are you happy? Of course, you nearly got yourself killed."

Sterling was picking up sadness from him, something deeply sullen and strikingly painful.

"There is inherent danger in this line of work, just as there is in police work." Aware of the old numbness rising to protect her, Sterling challenged its grip. More compelling, she let the sunlight of Ben's love warm her as she moved a step closer. "You almost get yourself killed every day you go to work. Why?"

"For people like you," he said, mirroring her step. "To keep the streets safe. So most days, no one loses a father, brother, or daughter."

Sterling bowed her head, her pulse racing with the echoes of all things lost. Maybe it wasn't too late for her either.

Ben lifted her chin up to face him. "What is it, Sterling?"

"Maybe you were right about some things, too." Her voice barely rose above a whisper. "What you do scares me. But I haven't been myself for a really long time. You've made me see that. It was all an illusion. Getting lost in the work, trying to control everything, it wasn't working. By trying to keep from getting hurt, I was letting the scumbags run my life. Maybe the only way I can be safe from pain is to take back my life. Maybe I can never be safe from pain, but maybe I can redefine pain to something tolerable and full of life."

Sterling felt all the negative forces she'd energized with her fears quaking insider her. She stood trembling before Ben, knowing she could either continue on listening to the litany of voices prompting her to isolate herself behind tall walls or she could let the walls crumble. It was so simple, but so hard.

Slowly, gently, Ben pulled her into his embrace. "Oh, Sterling. It's okay. For now, just let me hold you."

The constant beat of his heart pounded softly against her chest. It comforted her and drew her down to a point where everything contracted into truth and expanded into elation. "Please, don't ever let me go," she breathed.

Ben held her out at arm's length, staring down with baffled eyes. "You are okay, right?" Gently, he touched the knot on the side of her head. "That's a nasty bump Cummings gave you."

"Stop it, you nut," she said. "I'm fine. I'm just happy. Don't you want me to be happy?"

Ben's eyes shifted and concern knitted his brow. Dropping his grip on her arms, he walked across the room and stared into space. "You surely know I want you to be happy, Sterling."

"What's wrong?"

"What are we doing? For days you've been pushing me away, telling me there's no future for us. No happily-ever-after for people like us. Remember?" Turning, he thrust a darkly sad gaze on her. "Never let you go? God, Sterling, do you know how I've longed for you to say those very words? But what does it mean?"

Her pulse skiddering in her throat, Sterling went to him again. "Ben--" Sterling rested her hand on his arm and felt the warmth of it.

"You've made me see that the terrible things that shaped my life don't fit anymore. The aloneness, the deaths. They don't have to haunt me. But I can't help but wonder, what happens next? How long before you walk away, before I lose you again?"

"Ben," she repeated softly, putting her finger to his lips. "Don't say anything until I've finished, please." She had to say it all just right. "Lying there in that building, I knew it was only a matter of time before those men would end my life. I was terrified. I didn't want to die. But when I got past the fear of dying, everything unimportant fell away."

Standing so close she could feel Ben's warm breath on her cheek, Sterling peered into his eyes. She'd hurt him so much, could he ever trust her again? Fear clutched her heart. She had to make him see the truth as she did, like touching an icicle dangling from an eaves -- the coldness of it sucks the breath from your lungs, the exquisite beauty of its clarity brings all your senses into one focal point.

"I wanted to live, but I wanted to live to be with you, Ben. Always."

His left eyebrow lifted.

"I know you can't guarantee me I won't follow my family's legacy of death. I know if you and I commit to each other, I'm risking becoming a cop's widow. But life is made up of moments. The moment my father was taken from me left me with great pain. It's time I realized, like Lacey said, it's all part of living. And moments of great happiness count far more."

Ben closed his eyes and breathed in deeply. Sterling waited.

Then he exhaled, as though breathing out all the pain he'd felt in the last two years. Opening his eyes, Ben gazed down at her with the same warmth she'd always counted on. But it was so much more. "Does this mean you'll stay?"

"If you'll have me," Sterling managed to say over the lump in her throat.

Gentleness and sweetness swirled between them, melting her heart to his. Then suddenly Ben's arms swept around her, pulling her in hard. His mouth devoured hers hungrily.

Wetness touched her cheek. "Ben, you're crying," she said breaking from his kiss.

"You've always gotten to me, Sterling, I won't deny it. You're like breath to me. I need you, always," he said brushing away a matching tear from her cheek.

"You have me. Always."

EPILOGUE

Two years later ...

"You're doing great, Sterling," Ben said, gently wiping perspiration from her brow.

"Great? Are you kidding? This is very painful."

"Okay, Mrs. Kirby, another hard push and we're going to have a baby," said the doctor.

Gripping Ben's hands, Sterling pushed as hard as she could, pushing through the pain until jubilation of birth filled her.

"It's a boy!" cried the doctor. "I don't care how many times I've done this, each time I deliver a baby it feels like a miracle."

The nurse placed the baby in Sterling's arms. "Do you have a name picked out?"

"Joshua Jr.," Ben answered, pride shining from his face.

"Joshua Jr.," Sterling echoed. "That has a very nice ring to it. Life goes on." Sweet thoughts of her son's namesake warmed her heart. *I'm not so afraid anymore, Dad. I love you. Always.*

"He's beautiful, Sterling." Caressing Sterling's head, Ben added, "Guess we can add another precious moment to our life. And something tells me there's going to be plenty more."

Writing as Kelynn Storm

Touch of Breeze: The Common Elements Romance Project

Love Between Universes, An Out of this World Christmas

ABOUT THE AUTHOR

After cutting her writing teeth as a feature writer for commercial and trade magazines, a reporter for newspapers and radio, and an executive editor for a communications company, award-winning author Lynn Crandall tuned her voracious appetite for stories to writing contemporary and paranormal romance, women's fiction, and romantic suspense. In her books, she enjoys taking readers on emotional journeys with relatable characters who refuse to back down, and face challenges and tribulations with heart and soul. She believes every love has a story, and hers is with one handsome husband and a large, beautiful circle of family, including her cat Winter.

9 798991 468909